"Amateur Hour"

Johnny Boucher

Copyright 2020

Published in Santa Fe, New Mexico

All Rights Reserved

Cover Photo James Lilly
"Terry Lease Holding WW2 Radom "

D1247958

Amateur Hour
A Boston Crime Novel by Johnny Boucher
©2020

1

Tori pulled up to the curb and parked in front of an old triple decker house, its dark green paint flaking, a thin strip of lawn burned to brown straw by the summer sun. Her car, a brown station wagon with fake wood panelling on the sides, looked about the same.

"Someday," she said, "we're going to buy drugs from a supplier right in Boston. We won't have to drive out to these shithole neighborhoods like Mattapan any more."

She turned to look at Dave in the passenger seat. He was still, head leaning back on the headrest.

"David!" she said sharply.

He opened one eye and said "Mmmmm?"

"David for Christ fuck! Wake up!"

"I'm awake," he said quietly. His voice was low and thick.

"David," she said. "Do I ask you to do much on this job? All you have to do is stand around and look tough. If anybody fucks with me, you kill them. If anybody tries to steal my dope, you kill them. I let you stay at my place. I let you shoot my dope."

"Thank you," he said.

"The one thing I ask you to do," she said, "Is when we're buying drugs, to please not shoot so much dope that you can't!" She hit him on the shoulder with each word. "Keep! Your eyes! Fucking! Open!"

"I've got it," he said, catching her by the wrist. "I've got it. Can we get to work now?"

"Jesus," she said as they got out of the car. "Some hard guy you are. If I hadn't of reminded you, you would of forgot your fucking gun!"

"Will you relax?" Dave said. "Cyrus is your ex-boyfriend. He's not going to steal your money or cheat you on a deal. Jesus, T. You worry too much."

They crossed the street toward the green house.

"Worry too much, he says," she said. "Of course I fucking worry. Do you know how long I'm going to jail for if I get popped again for dealing? And do you think you're helping things, with your eyes half shut half the time? Drooling like a fucking retard? And for Christ fuck, the suit and the hair down to your shoulders have to go. You look like a fucking drug dealer from the nineties."

"Tori. I am a drug dealer from the nineties. And I always will be."

They went up the steps and Tori knocked on the door. Dave looked at her face in the sunlight. The years were starting to tell on her like they did on everyone, but she was still a beautiful girl. Drugs hadn't destroyed her skin like they did some chicks. With her black jeans, black jean jacket, and black hair, she looked like a badass rock and roll singer. She was always saying she would get a band together one of these days. Sometimes she would sit for hours watching old episodes of Behind The Music. The rock stars with their outrageous drug habits made her laugh. When the end of the show came and they either quit drugs or died, she would grab the remote and fast forward over that part.

"What did you say?" she said.

"I said you're a ball-busting pain in my prick. And I resent that about looking like a drug dealer. This is an Armani one-fucking-button fucking tan linen suit. It's the height of warm weather elegance."

"Hmm," she said. "And the black shirt and tie are supposed to make you look like some kind of mafia assassin?"

"Say what you want about the mafia," he said. "They understand the importance of a dress code."

He settled his pistol in the front of his belt. Tori had gotten it for him, an elegant gun, Italian, a Beretta, stainless steel finish, not the same old chunky black Glock 17 that the cops and the young gangbangers all carried. It made him laugh, the way everyone nowadays used the same equipment. A cop had to carry the gun he was issued, and the Glock was a reliable working pistol. But in crime you could carry any gun you wanted. Why get a boring old Glock when you could carry an HK. A Ruger. A Steyr-Aug. A Sig-Sauer. A Walther. And those were only the ones from Germany.

He liked the Beretta. It was an excellent gun and a work of art. Tori was a lot to take, but you had to respect a woman who left a Beretta 92F, two spare clips, and a hundred rounds of 9 millimeter ammunition for you under the Christmas tree.

"Oh, cut it out," Tori said. "I see you looking at yourself in the window glass. You're worse than a girl. Are you sure you're not gay? You're really too good-looking to be straight."

"Uh… thanks."

A young white guy with dreadlocks and a goatee, wearing a tie-dye t-shirt, tattered jeans, and sandals, opened the door. He said "Hey" to Tori and nodded to Dave.

They walked through an entryway, its white paint gone gray with age. An old dark green ten-speed bike leaned against the wall, always in the same position. Dave stepped carefully past it. He had brushed up against it once and come away with a smear of dust, rust, and oil that had ruined his jacket.

Dave hung back, making sure the butt of the pistol showed above his crossed hands, as Tori and the Kid walked into the living room. Thin blades of sunlight stabbed into the room through the blinds, lighting up grains of dust that swarmed in the air like a million tiny fireflies. Wallpaper that had once been a bright yellow with blue singing birds showed dimly through a coating of grime. From a rusty metal stand in the corner hung a spider plant. Tori had told him once that spider plants were perfect for people who weren't good with plants, that they were almost impossible to kill. This one was dead.

A low couch and two matching easy chairs, upholstered in what looked like a homeless guy's overcoat, slumped on the scraped wooden floor. Between them stood a coffee table, its top crowded with cigarette burns and hundreds of boldly printed moisture rings where drinks had sat on a finish that had given up in disgust decades before.

Cyrus came into the room, said "Hey, baby" to Tori, and nodded to Dave. He was a fortyish black guy with a shaved head in an olive-colored linen double-breasted suit, a white silk shirt, and two-tone wingtips, white and brown. The buttons on the jacket were made of some kind of shimmery mother-of-pearl-looking plastic. Dave wondered if they had come with the jacket or if Cyrus had had his tailor sew them on.

Cyrus and Tori went to work. He gave her a brown paper lunch bag and she gave him a wad of money. He started counting it, not much, a couple of thousand today, and she quickly counted over the neatly wrapped packages. The dope was already in bundles by the time it got to this house, always the same dope, so there was never any shit about purity or measurements to talk about, just the right number of bundles.

As Cyrus counted, he glanced up at Dave.

"What you looking at, David?"

"Huh?" Dave said. "Oh. I was just looking at your suit. It's funny. That color green always looks great on black guys, but if a white guy wears it, it just makes him look sick to his stomach. And your head. I was just thinking, why is it that a black guy with a shaved head always looks cool, but a white guy with a shaved head just looks… bald?"

"You one of a kind, my man," Cyrus said. He turned to Tori, who counted bundles, silently shaking her head. "Where you hire your employees at, girl?"

"Don't even get me started," she said. She counted over the last few bundles and looked up.

"Okay," she said. "We're good. We'll talk to you later."

"All right," Cyrus said, and nodded, with a tiny smile, to Dave. Dave opened the door for Tori and she walked out. He waited for a few seconds, nodded, and pulled the door shut behind him.

"Hurry up," Tori said, getting into the passenger seat. Dave started the car and pulled away from the curb.

"What?" she said.

"What?"

"You're mumbling to yourself," she said.

"I said what do you got to bust my balls about my hair? It took me two fucking years to grow it long. You didn't know me those first couple of years when it was all those in-between lengths, when it looked completely gay, all pasted down with gel. So I finally get it to where it looks good and now I got to get my fucking balls busted about it? What? What the fuck is so funny?"

"Cyrus was right," she said, smiling. "You one of a kind, my man."

They went through Cambridge first, Central Square, Dave calling ahead to let the customers know they were coming. A waitress bought three bundles, three hundred dollars. She was getting serious and was starting to buy most days. Next was a sick girl trying to get off dope, eating valiums and drinking vodka to try to make it through but still puking and shitting and shaking and crying and just needing a little bit this one last time. Two bags. Twenty dollars. Nineteen, actually. They let her slide on the one dollar. Dave even gave her a cigarette. He felt bad for her, but business was business. No one held a gun to this girl's head and made her shoot dope. And no one forced him and Tori to risk going to jail to sell a chickenshit nineteen dollars' worth of heroin, but there it was. This was America. People were going to do what they were going to do. As Tori had a very bad habit of saying to cops and prosecuting attorneys, "Next fucking question?"

It was getting two o'clock when they pulled onto the Mass Ave bridge, Tori at the wheel, to cross the Charles River into the Back Bay. A painter, a designer, fags like that, were waiting with good money for decent amounts of dope. Now they would make some cash, go home and shoot some more dope, and wait for calls to go out and sell more dope.

They were most of the way over the bridge when the light at the end turned red and cars started to slow down. Behind them a siren started up. Dave had supersized his wakeup shot in the morning and was still pretty high, but he pulled himself together fast. Looking back, he saw a hand reach up and put one of those little red flashing lights on the roof of a car.

"Fuckfuckfuckmotherfuck!" Tori said. There were a few car lengths of open road in front of her. She gunned the engine as if she could get away somehow through all the cars stopped at the light.

Dave pulled the Beretta out of his waistband and threw it hard straight out the window. It wheeled, like a boomerang, through the air, in slow motion, sunlight glinting off the beautiful chrome finish, so bright Dave thought everyone in Boston could see it, cleared the railing, and disappeared over the side of the bridge.

Tori slammed on the brakes as they came up to the cars stopped at the light. She looked around, trapped but still trying to think. It was no good. Traffic was solid through the intersection ahead, the sidewalk of the bridge was too narrow, and the cop car pulled up on her left rear corner, boxing her in. She started stuffing bundles of dope into her pants. Dave laughed. It was over. He put his hands slowly on the dashboard.

2

Detox wasn't so bad. Dave tried to tell himself so every time he landed in detox. It wasn't true this time either. Detox was a stone drag. There was nothing to do but think about all the terrible things you didn't have to think about when you were on dope, like being without dope, for example.

Or life. That was always a depressing thing to think about. Without drugs to smooth things out, you were back to the same old shit you had tried to escape from with drugs, the same raw deal that there wasn't even anyone to blame for. There was nowhere to hide, no safe place, wherever you went. The world was a prison where you counted out your sentence the best you could. Sure, there was no door on your cell, and you could break the rules all you wanted. What could they do to you if you were already in prison? But you could never forget the miserable hole you were in. Where you were going to stay. Forever.

He knew if he started thinking he would just tear himself up over things he couldn't change. There was nothing to gain that way. He was stuck here with no dope and just his thoughts. So he thought about dope. He thought how lucky he was to have big veins, like bicycle tires, in his arms, what they called junkie porn. He thought about the little sound, the tiny snick, that a needle made when it poked through the skin of your arm. How you knew you had a vein when you pulled the plunger back and the blood came out into the barrel of the needle, fast at first, then, when you stopped pulling, slow, mixing in with the dope in the needle, swishing back and forth, like a wave in the ocean, while you got your thumb on the hammer and started slowly pushing, sending the blood back in and behind it the dope. He thought about the nuns when he was a kid had tried to teach him about sacraments. Like they knew fuck what a sacrament really was. He wondered how many people he would have to tell that he wouldn't shoot dope any more before he could get the fuck out of here and shoot some fucking dope.

3

Dave was sitting up in bed, not feeling that bad, considering, when his lawyer came in.

"David!" the lawyer called in his big gay voice.

"Thomas," Dave said, smiling a little. Thomas was a piece of work. What his mother would have called a fancypants. The first thing he made clear when he met you was that he liked to be called Thomas, not Tom, and especially not Tommy.

Thomas looked cool, like he always did, and rich, though he was only a public defender. He had on a suit, a nubbly silvery silk thing with a tiny pink stripe, and little gray loafers. Dave wondered why, with all the jokes about gay guys being light in the loafers, every homo you saw had on loafers.

Thomas pulled a chair up to Dave's bed, sat down, and crossed his legs, setting down his briefcase, which was gray leather and matched his shoes and his belt, and smiling his big gay smile.

"David," he said again.

"Thomas," Dave said. "You're gay. You must know this. I was just wondering why it is that all of you talk the same way, with that, you know, gay accent. I mean, is it something you learn, or are you born talking like. You know. You."

Thomas stared for a minute.

"I can never tell with you, David," he said. "Sometimes I think you're very intelligent. Other times I think you have no idea what you're saying. Like a child. Or a retarded person."

"I don't understand the question," Dave said.

"Never mind, David," Thomas said, clapping his hands together. "On to business. Good news first or bad?"

"You pick," Dave said.

"Mr. Playful today."

"Come on, Thomas," Dave said. "Don't yank my yodel."

"All right," Thomas said. "Bad news first. Your girlfriend is going to do some time. Her history, the amount she had stuffed in her pants, she's retired. I'm sorry, David."

Dave sat perfectly still. He knew Thomas would feel they had to look solemn in honor of Tori. Dave hoped it wouldn't last too long.

"You, though," Thomas said, "are a lucky young man. The cops know you were working with her. Your statement that she picked you up hitchhiking didn't make much of an impression. But none of the criminal enterprise stuff, the car, the apartment, the phone, nothing's in your name. You didn't have any drugs on you yourself, although the police lab tech's report said the level of opiates in your blood was – I think the word he used was 'titanic.' They've got no case beyond your being there. I met with the district attorney's people and really played up your military service. I made you into quite a hero."

"Thomas, I was thrown out of the Army for selling heroin. They know that."

"Well, yes, but your record is clean since then, and I pitched you as a confused young ex-soldier trying to find his way in the bewildering world of civilian life and falling in with the wrong element."

"They bought it?" Dave asked.

"I wouldn't say that. They laughed pretty hard. But I kept talking and talking and I wore them down. The DA's got other things on his mind now anyway. He's all excited about his new campaign to fry everyone they catch with an illegal handgun."

Dave smiled. They hadn't seen the gun. Luck. Dumb luck. You just never knew sometimes.

"Anyway," Thomas went on, "after you finish up here it's rehab, then probation. Get a job, stay off drugs, and you could come out of this all right. But if you get into trouble again it'll be prison for you, too, David. I won't be able to help you."

Thomas put on a concerned look.

"David, talk to me. I'm your lawyer. I'll do the best I can for you. But what are you thinking? You're smart. You're young. You're good-looking. You don't have to live this way. What do you really want to do?"

"I don't know, Thomas," he said. "What kind of question is that? I'll... get back to you."

Thomas looked hesitant, then said "David, why don't you come to work for me?"

"As what?" Dave asked.

"As a law clerk."

"Law clerk? You mean as a secretary?" Dave asked.

"David," Thomas said, "if you don't start somewhere, what do you think is going to happen to you? What kind of job are you going to get with your record? What do you know how to do? I know what you're good at. The same things I'm good at. Driving around, wearing expensive clothes, and talking a lot of shit. You're a natural, David."

"You've got a point," Dave said.

"The law is a good life, David. It's exciting. There's something different every day. You need to see a different side of life. I could show it to you."

"I don't know anything about the law, Thomas," Dave said. "Except how to break it. How would – "

"David. David. Don't tell me why it wouldn't work. It will work. Listen. This is our plan. We'll get you out of here and into a methadone program. You'll start working with me, in, well, yes, a clerical capacity, just at first, while we get you started in night school to get your paralegal certificate. I'll – "

"Thomas, I appreciate – "

"David! I'm offering you a way out. A chance to start over. To build a career. To make a life. Think, David. How often does an offer like that come along?"

Dave tried to answer. He had to admit that he was speechless.

.45

The day finally came for Dave to be released from rehab, but the paperwork was fucked up somewhere along the line. He could feel his blood boil and his fists clench. He took some deep breaths and tried to be calm. It was no use getting bent out of shape. No one would listen. No one cared about him or his problems. He hung his suit back up in the closet in his room and went to bed. Dinner didn't interest him. It was chicken again. He wondered why they always, always served chicken in rehab. He had asked, but no one knew.

The night was long. He lay in bed sweating, whipped by panic like a shirt on a clothesline. He had been able to get through by counting the days until he got out. Now here was another. He could feel his mind start to race ahead into the future, to imagine how badly things could go. He worried that his release paperwork would be lost. He worried that his case would be forgotten. He worried that he would be stuck in here. Christ, rehab was worse than jail. In jail you could at least get dope.

As his anxiety spun out of control, he felt the insane rage he always felt when he couldn't stop himself from worrying. Other people inherited being smart or good at sports. He had inherited an imagination that made a list of every terrible thing that could happen. It was a sickness. His mother's side of the family had poisoned his blood with it. He knew he would have worried himself to death years ago if he hadn't been lucky enough to find the antidote. When he shot a big spoonful of dope, all that worry stopped. After all these years it still worked, just like shutting off a switch. With an armful, life was fine. He was free. There was nothing to fear. Nothing bad could happen. And if it did, who gave a fuck?

In the morning his papers came in and they cut him loose. It was a sunny day outside, too hot for his suit, but he liked this weather. Summer in Boston was too short to get tired of. He felt like slapping people who griped that it was too hot. They were always the same pricks who griped that it was too cold the other ten months. One of these days he would leave. Go where there was more summer. South, to Austin. West, maybe. Phoenix. He smiled to himself in the sunlight. Sure. One of these days he was going to give up drugs and crime, too.

He went to the bank, took out the last of his money, and got his other gun from his safe deposit box. There was supposed to be a thousand dollars and a bundle of dope in there for emergencies. He had long since shot the dope and spent the thousand, on dope, but the gun was there.

Holding the pistol in his hand made him happy. The Beretta Tori had given him was nice, but there was something noble, patriotic, something clean, about a Colt .45. American fighting men had relied on it since before he was born. It was a piece of history. Besides, the private eye on his favorite teevee show, Magnum, PI, carried one. With that name, you would think he would carry a Magnum. Or be named .45, and the show be called .45, PI, but .45 wasn't a real person's name, although, come to think of it, neither was Magnum.

Dave looked at his watch. It was a Swatch, a yellow plastic thing he had stolen from some chick, one of the counselors in rehab. It was humiliating to wear such a faggot piece of shit, but he hadn't had time to steal anything better. Looking at the stupid little plastic dial, he saw that there wasn't time for everything on his list of things to do. He was going to miss visiting hours at the jail where they were holding Tori. He felt bad that he wouldn't be able to see her. But it was a lose-lose situation. If he saw her, he'd feel bad, too. Still, there was still enough of the day left for things to go his way. He slid the .45 under his belt, walked out to the street, and got a cab for Mattapan.

.40

Dave knocked on the door and stepped back on the porch so they could see it was him. He saw the Kid's face through the window and heard him telling Cyrus who it was and Cyrus saying let him in, let him in.

"Hey, man," the Kid said, opening the door. The Kid had on the same ratty jeans and tie-dye t-shirt he always seemed to be wearing. The same green bicycle was in its place by the door. The same dust floated in the air.

"Kid," Dave said, walking in. Cyrus was sitting on the couch in the living room. He was wearing loafers, jeans, and a wife-beater.

"Cyrus," Dave said.

"David, welcome," Cyrus said. "Nice watch."

"We heard about Tori," the Kid said, closing and locking the front door.

"Yeah," Dave said. "Yeah, they set her court date."

"She's not too happy about that, I suppose," said Cyrus.

"No," Dave said. "No, but you know her. She's going to promise to stay off dope if they let her go live with her father."

Cyrus laughed. Dave laughed. The Kid looked puzzled. Cyrus told him "Kid, Tori talks this same shit every time she gets in trouble, that she's going to go to her father, to be safe from drugs, like he lives in Montana or some shit. Tori's father lives in Los Angeles."

The Kid smiled and shook his head. He folded his arms and leaned against the living room door frame. Dave sat in the easy chair across from Cyrus.

"David," Cyrus said, businesslike. "What can we do for you today?"

"Well, I'd like to get back to work," Dave said. "I've been back in touch with the clients Tori and I had. Everybody's real sad what happened to her, but they're ready to do business with me."

"That's good," Cyrus said, nodding, "that's very good. How much would you like to buy today?"

Dave smiled. Cyrus didn't smile.

"Well," Dave said, "Let's talk about that. The cops took all the dope and the money Tori and I had. I got a couple of hundred bucks on me now that I can put down as, you know, a good faith deposit, but the thing is I've talked to my clients and I've got a full day of deliveries lined up. If you'll front me the stuff, I'll have the money back here by the end of the day, and whatever profit I've made you know I'm going to spend with you on more dope. We can do good business together if you can just start me off today."

Cyrus shook his head.

"David, David, my man, you're embarrassing me. You know I don't give credit. I didn't even give it to Tori, and Tori and I went way back. I'll give you as much dope as you can afford to buy in cash today. You sell that and come back with some money, and I'll sell you some more dope. I understand your trouble, but I can't go changing my business practices on account of your misfortune."

"Listen, man, come on," Dave said. "You've got me by the ball bag here, Cyrus. I'm talking to you man to man. I need one day to get back on my feet and then I'll be out there selling your dope, working like a nigger for you. A few hours to get started is all I'm asking for. A few bags of dope. Whose dick do I have to suck over here? Come on, man."

Cyrus said "David, David. I understand your position and I sympathize. I would hope you could understand my position, but if you can't, well, I may feel a little disappointed, but I'll get over that. You came here to buy narcotics, David. Now, do you want to buy what you can afford right now, today, and leave my house, or do you just want to leave my house?"

Dave sighed and leaned back in his chair. His jacket fell open to the side and the butt of his pistol showed. He had polished the gun in the cab with one of his socks. A ray of sunlight sparkled off the metal. Cyrus' eyes flashed from the pistol over to the Kid. The Kid pulled his pistol out of the front of his pants and pointed it at Dave. It was a Colt Python, .357 magnum, stainless steel finish, four-inch barrel, with a vented rib. Though the Kid had put fancy tiger-stripe cocobolo-wood handgrips on it, this gun was all business. Dave looked, surprised, from Cyrus over at the Kid.

"What the fuck?" Dave said. "What the fuck are you guys doing? I'm trying to talk business here. Jesus, if we can't agree on something, fine, we can't agree on something, but you got no call to be pulling guns on people. I mean all right, okay, you win. It's your dope, you won't front it to me, fine. You're the boss. We'll do it your way. I'd like to buy as much dope as I can afford to buy in cash, right now, today, then I'll leave your house. I'll have to start smaller than I was hoping for, I mean it's going to take me forfuckin'ever at this rate, but I'll sell it and make some money and I'll be back for more and eventually we'll get some business moving here. For Christ's fuck, Cy. The fuck are you thinking?"

Cyrus looked at Dave. "David, do me a favor and slowly take your gun out and put it on the couch."

Dave rolled his eyes and sighed. He took his gun out and tossed it on the couch. From the coffee table he picked up a pack of Kools and a lighter. Cyrus sat, looking at him. Dave looked back at the Kid, who was standing in the doorway, still pointing his gun.

"Hey, Kid. Let me ask you a question."

Dave lit a cigarette.

"What?" the Kid said.

"Did Tori ever mention to you guys that I ever shot anybody?"

The Kid paused. "I don't know. I don't think so."

"Have you ever seen me fire a gun?"

"No."

"Have you ever seen me take my gun out before today?"

"No."

"All right. Let me ask you another question. Do you ever get nervous carrying a gun in your pants that someday you're going to blow your balls off?"

"Well. Yeah. I guess."

"Did you ever think maybe it would be safer if you just carried the gun around with no bullets in it?"

"What good's a gun with no bullets in it?" the Kid asked.

"Well, for shooting people, it wouldn't be any good at all. But if, let's say, you know, just for example, you had a job where you carried a gun, and on this job you saw the same people all the time, and you felt pretty sure you weren't going to be shooting anybody, and nobody was going to be shooting you, and it was a good job, but to keep this job you had to let a certain person believe that, if anything happened, you were ready to protect her, and start shooting everybody. Well, let's say you stopped, one day, worrying, about shooting people, about people shooting you, about shooting your own balls off, and just stopped loading the gun, and started just carrying it around, unloaded, would you go and tell that to the person you were supposed to be protecting? Would you tell anyone? I mean, you'd be pretty embarrassed to admit a thing like that, wouldn't you? It would make you look like an asshole, wouldn't it? Wouldn't it?"

"Uh... yeah," the Kid said.

"Of course it would," Dave said. "But I'll tell you, I'd rather look like an asshole than have you shoot me right now over a gun with no fucking bullets in it. Now, if the two of you are ready to put your dicks away, can we get back to business here?"

Cyrus stared at Dave. Dave looked calmly back and forth from Cyrus to the Kid. The Kid looked back and forth from Cyrus to Dave. Then Cyrus smiled and slowly started to laugh.

"Shit," he said. "Shit, man. I told her it was all downhill after me, and god damn me if I wasn't right. An empty gun? You walk around with an empty motherfucking gun?"

Dave smiled. "I said I'm embarrassed. I admit it, I'm embarrassed. Come on, man. Give me a break. Can we talk about something else?"

Cyrus laughed. The Kid smiled, put his gun back in his pants and, crossing his arms, leaned back against the doorframe. Dave leaned forward, tapping his cigarette in the ashtray.

Cyrus looked from Dave to the gun on the couch and stopped laughing.

"Still," Cyrus said, and started to reach for the gun. Dave dropped his cigarette, grabbed the gun, shot Cyrus once in the chest, spun around and shot the Kid in the face, then turned back and shot Cyrus again through the heart. Cyrus sat, eyes open, staring, like he was about to say something. Dave sat, still pointing the gun at Cyrus, listening to the huge ringing silence.

Dave got up and looked at his watch. He took the watch off, dropped it on the floor, stomped on it, yanked the big chunky gold Breitling Windrider chronograph off Cyrus' wrist, put it on, and checked the time. He went through Cyrus' and the Kid's pockets and took their wallets, Cyrus' car keys, and the Kid's gun. He quickly ran upstairs, kicking open doors, the .45 in his right hand and the Kid's magnum in his left. There was no one.

Upstairs, the place was neat and clean, like a barracks. One room had a bed, a dresser, a weight bench, and a TV running with the sound off. The picture showed a living room with a dead guy in a chair and another on the floor. Dave looked closer. It was Cyrus and the Kid.

He found the DVD deck connected to the television. He took the DVD out and put it in his jacket pocket.

In the next room, a canvas carry bag sat on a table. Dave looked into it and stopped in his tracks. The bag was full of dope, so much dope it didn't even look real. If ten bags made a bundle, five bundles made a brick, two bricks made a package, and five packages made a block, this was a whole city. He felt dizzy, and he realized he had stopped breathing. He picked up the bag and slung it over his shoulder.

He tore through all the dressers and closets. He found a carton of cigarettes, a bag of cash, some loose, some large bills in big stacks, a bag of clean needles, and a couple of shoeboxes full of huge bottles of tranquilizers and painkillers and muscle relaxants. He found a pistol-grip shotgun in a closet, with boxes of 12-gauge shells, and five bags of bullets for the magnum, a hundred in each bag. He found a little chrome .25 automatic in a black nylon ankle holster under the pillow of one of the beds. He found a big black duffel bag in another closet. It was full of expensive workout clothes that had never been worn. The receipt was still in there, from a year before. He dumped the sweats on the floor and packed up the drugs, the guns, and a stack of DVDs he found in the closet, and zipped up the bag. He looked at his watch again. Three and a half minutes. In Mattapan the cops might show up at a shooting sooner, later, or not at all. He didn't feel like waiting to see which.

He slung the bag over his shoulder and ran down the stairs to the front door. As he passed the Kid's body, he stopped.

"Point a fucking gun at me?" he said. "Didn't I tell you nobody points a fucking gun at me? Huh? That means nobody!" He kicked the Kid hard in the stomach. "And get a haircut, faggot!"

He walked out onto the porch and looked around the neighborhood. Nothing moved. He opened the door, walked back in, and kicked over the green bike. It clattered to the floor in a cloud of dust. Then he walked over to Cyrus and shot him again.

Cyrus' car was parked out in front of the house. Dave got in and took off fast, but not fast enough to look like he was fleeing a crime scene. The car was a Mercedes convertible, silver, nice car, but the glare of the sun off the hood was blinding. He put on a pair of wraparound sunglasses he found on the dashboard. Looking in the rearview mirror for cops, he caught his reflection and had to laugh. In this suit and the sunglasses, he looked like a heavily armed Beatle.

.44

Dave parked Cyrus' car in the South End, carefully wiped his prints off the steering wheel and the door handle, and walked over to the Midtown Motor Inn. The Midtown was his favorite. He loved the smell of it, the hotel smell, the smell of flowers and dust and exhausted rugs. He loved the piles of clean towels that appeared every morning, like magic, no matter what godawful filth you had gotten on them the night before. He loved the tiny soaps in the bathrooms, like hotel guests were all midgets. Living in hotels made him feel like a king, even if it was only the king of midgets.

He got a room on the second floor. Second floors were good. First floors weren't good. Guys could walk straight into a first-floor room from outside, like those fucking Army narc motherfuckers had. Three years it had been, and it still made him sick with anger to remember the smug looks on their pink faces as they handcuffed him and slapped a big evidence tag on the duffel bag full of dope he had. The Dutch courier had gotten away, or maybe he had tipped the Americans off in the first place.

They wouldn't even let him shoot up before they hauled him away. They treated him like he had done something wrong. They were the ones ruining a guy's career. He had really been going places in the military, giving the soldiers what they wanted, a little taste of home. The money he was making doing it was outrageous. He was clearing more than his commanding officer did, and he was only a private.

Closing the blinds, he emptied the duffel bag out onto the bed and looked over his haul. He could hardly believe it. There were enough weapons and narcotics here to send him to jail for a thousand years. It was nerve racking. But he knew the best way to relax in the world. He looked over all the dope he had and reminded himself he had to be careful. His tolerance was gone, after detox and rehab. He could easily OD. He didn't want that to happen, not when for the first time in his life he had all the dope and money he wanted. He decided he had better start building up his resistance. He had better start right away.

.32

Dave drove down the Jamaicaway, smiling, the wind blowing through his hair. He hated the J-way. Everyone did. It was a narrow, winding strip of road that ran from town all the way down to Jamaica Plain, full of hills and dips and sudden blind corners. Yet everyone drove as fast as they could, like it was a highway, swerving into your lane like you weren't even there. But fuck it. Nothing was going to ruin his mood today.

He reminded himself as he drove that he should ditch Cyrus' car for good, maybe later on in the day. Then again, he had found it that morning right where he left it the day before. Maybe the cops weren't looking for it.

He drove through Roslindale Square and up Belgrade Ave. He tried to keep memories from running through his mind, but he couldn't help it. His grandparents had lived on this street. Visiting them when he was a kid had been an escape from the fearful North Shore streets of Lynn where his family lived. The big sitting room in the front of the house was wallpapered with a huge panoramic scene of a bay in China, with sailboats, junks, they were called, and peasants driving carts pulled by huge water buffaloes. His grandfather, who had worked as a paperhanger when he was young, had hung it himself. Dave remembered how he would stare at the wallpaper, imagining he was there, far away, in China, imagining that he could escape.

Dave liked his grandfather, Leo. Leo was a peaceful old guy. He didn't say much, but he always seemed happy. He was the first dope fiend Dave had ever seen.

Leo's drugs were prescribed for him. He needed to dissolve extract of opium in a glass of water and drink it three times a day. Doctor's orders. Something about his guts. He was so high he could look down and see kites. He had sat that way in his ratty old rocking chair for longer than Dave had been alive, glassy-eyed, motionless, too smacked out even to rock. It looked like fun. If the old guy ever noticed that his bottle of opium extract was a few drops short every time little Davey and his folks visited, he never said so.

Dave parked outside Tori's mother's house and walked up the front steps. Through the screen door he could hear the teevee.

"Eileen?" he called.

"Come in, David," she said.

He opened the door and walked into the living room. Eileen was sitting in a recliner in shorts and a t-shirt, smoking a cigarette and drinking a beer. He was a little startled, like he always was when he saw her. She looked like Tori. Not like Tori's mother or even like Tori's older sister. Exactly like Tori. She turned off the teevee with the remote and looked at him.

"We heard you got out," she said. Her voice was cold.

Dave shrugged.

"I was lucky," he said. "They knew it was Tori's show and I was just security."

"Security," she said. "Nice job, Mr. Security. I'm sure Tori will give you a good recommendation. You were supposed to protect my daughter, David. You should have shot those cops."

"Dealers," he said. "I was supposed to shoot dealers. If they tried to cheat her. Or customers. If they tried to rob her. There was nothing in my job prescription about shooting cops."

"What are you doing out of jail, anyway?" she asked. "You had a gun. That's a crime."

"I ditched the gun, Eileen. Didn't Tori tell you that?"

"No," she said. "I guess she was too busy trying to get away to pay attention to you. She said your ass just sat there like a fucking bump on a log. Security. Hah."

Dave shrugged again. He walked into the kitchen and got two Bud tallboys from the fridge. He gave her one, opened the other, and sat down on the couch.

"Listen, Eileen. Bust my balls if you want. What's done is done. How is Tori making out?"

"What's done is done, he says," she said. "How do you think she's 'making out,' David? She's in jail. My baby is in jail and she's going to stay in jail. They set her bail so high I can't even get her out so she can - "

Eileen stopped.

"So she can what?" Dave asked.

"Nothing," Eileen said.

"Eileen?"

"David."

"Eileen?"

"Yes, David?"

"Why are you looking at me like that, Eileen?"

"Like what, David?"

"Eileen, why are you staring at my jacket?"

"It's a nice jacket, David."

He stared at her, then shook his head.

"Eileen, you're something else."

"What do you mean, David?"

"Jesus fucking Christ, Eileen. I'm not wearing a fucking wire. I'm not working with the cops. I had my lawyer make a few calls, so I know you haven't been able to make her bail."

Dave took an envelope out of his jacket pocket and handed it to her. She opened it and counted the bills.

"Where did you get this?" she asked.

"Never mind where I got it," he said. "It should be enough to make her bond and leave her a little traveling money. She's finished in Boston. You know it. She knows it. She's got to jump bail and leave town right away. As soon as you get her out of jail. Tonight would be good. She can't fuck around. And she can't come back here, ever. If you want to see her again after this, you should think about going with her. So. Do you still think I'm working with the fucking cops? What about you, Eileen? Should I pat you down for a wire?"

"There's no need to be a smartass, David," she said.

"Jesus," he said.

"David, why are you doing this?" she asked.

"What do you mean, why am I doing this? Tori's... Tori. We were partners. She always did right by me. I want to do right by her. But she's got to trust me on this. The problems she already has are bad enough, but the cops are going to be coming around to question her about something new, a shooting, that involves people we used to do business with. Believe me, she doesn't want to get mixed up in this. The faster she gets away from all this and the farther she goes, the better off she'll be."

Eileen stared at him, then looked down at the money.

"I'm sorry, David," she said quietly. "I shouldn't have said what I said. Thank you for what you're doing for my baby. I know you love her too."

"Well," Dave said. "Let's not get carried away."

.50

Dave was trapped in a dream and couldn't get out. They were coming for him. He ran and he fell and he crawled, but they were right behind him. Finally he raced up the stairs to his room, slammed the door behind him, yanked open a dresser drawer, and got his gun. He could hear their footsteps thundering up the stairs. He checked the gun. It was empty. He scrambled around the bottom of the drawer and found some bullets, but the shells were all different sizes, and he couldn't tell in the dark which ones went with the gun. He tried the bullets one after another, his hands shaking like crazy, but none would fit in the chamber. The door jumped on its hinges as they kicked at it. Just as the lock gave way and the door swung open, he found a bullet that fit, slid it into the chamber, and snapped the cylinder shut. He turned to face them as they came toward him across the room, pointed the gun, and pulled the trigger. Nothing happened. He pulled the trigger again. There was a pitiful little popping sound. The bullet oozed out of the barrel, flew in slow motion for a few inches, then fell rattling onto the floor. By that time they were on him, and he screamed and screamed and woke up making little whimpering noises, like a cat.

"Son of a bitch," he said. "Jesus motherfuck."

He poured a sandwich bag of dope out onto the night table, rolled up a dollar, and snorted a big pile of powder. While he waited, he shook his head in disgust. Why did he still dream that dream? No one came after him or threatened him. Not any more. If they tried, he killed them. Those were the rules. It was good to have rules. It made life simple. No questions. No fear. But no one had explained that to his dreams.

.223

Dave sat looking at the teevee. He would get up in a while and turn it on. He was pretty high but his mind was still working, still thinking. He couldn't shake off the black mood his dream had brought.

He asked himself what the fuck. He had money. He had drugs. All the time-wasting bullshit, all the needing drugs and buying drugs and selling drugs for money to buy drugs, he was done with all that shit. He could sit and do nothing all day except drugs. He could enjoy himself. What did he I care what bullshit his homo lawyer said? Why did he have to decide what his life was about? Who the fuck passed a law that your life had to be "about" something? Fuck.

He found the remote and turned on the teevee, slowly clicking through channel after channel, finding nothing. He missed Tori suddenly. He remembered how they would shoot dope then sit up in bed and watch his collection of hard-guy action videos, one after another. She called it the Handgun Violence Channel and made up a slogan, All Handgun Violence All The Time.

He slowly shook his head. Thinking about her wouldn't change anything. Thinking was a dead end. A waste of time. He went back to clicking through the channels. He stopped when he found a channel running all the old private detective shows he had loved as a kid, one after another. Rockford, the trailer park detective. Cannon, the fatso detective. Magnum PI, the beach bum detective. This was more like it. He put the remote down on the floor and got ready to watch his shows. He felt his mood lifting. He smiled a little.

Then it came to him. In a flash it all played out in front of him. He felt stunned. It was perfect. It was fucking peerless genius. The best idea of his career, of his life. What was to stop him? What did you need? Balls? Had them. Guns? Had them. Brains? Well. He had guns.

It took him a few tries, but he stood up. He wiped dried blood off his arm with one of the hotel's nice clean white towels, got dressed, and went out. He bought a prepaid phone, put ads in the Phoenix and the Globe, and ordered a box of business cards at the office supply.

.357

Dave parked the Mercedes in an underground garage on Newbury Street and walked over to Copley Square. The bars on Boylston Street were mostly empty. These places would fill up with business people when the offices let out, but it was only three o'clock.

As he pushed open the door to some place, whichever one she had said, the air conditioning hit him like walking through a sprinkler on somebody's lawn. A shiver ran down his spine and the hair stood up on the back of his neck. A long bar ran down one side of the place, tables along the other. Homo piano music played softly in the background.

"I don't know why I wore a suit in this heat," a red-haired woman said to the bartender as he brought her a glass of white wine. "I look like I'm dressed for a job interview."

"Maureen Sheehan?" he said.

She turned and smiled at him. "Leo Diamond," she said. "Private Detective."

"Thanks for coming into town," he said. "I would of came out to Saugus."

"I know," she said. "But I needed to get out anyway. I'm driving myself nuts sitting at home worrying."

He sat next to her at the bar and asked for a club soda.

"I have to ask you," she said. She had a mild North Shore townie accent. Ahsk you. "Your name isn't really Leo Diamond, is it?"

"Well," he said. "It was better than the first one I made up."

"What was that?"

"Glen Plaid."

"Yeah. I guess it is." She looked at his face. "Listen," she said. "It's none of my business, but what's with your eye?"

"What eye?"

"Your left eye," she said. "It's half shut, like you're falling asleep."

"Oh," he said. "That eye. It's, uh. You know. Work-related."

"Work-related," she said. "A private eye injury?"

"That's a good one," he said. "Can I have one of your cigarettes?"

"So," she said. "I've never met a detective before. How did you get into this line of work?"

"Long story," he said. "Some of the guys who do it are ex-military or ex-cops, or both. I was in Army intelligence at shape – "

"What do you mean, at shape?" she asked.

"Oh," he said. "Sorry. SHAPE. Supreme Headquarters Allied Presence Europe. I was in Germany. Town of Heidelberg. Beautiful town."

"Why did you leave?" she asked.

"I ask myself that sometimes," he said. "I liked it there. But, you know, things don't always go like you plan. So here I am."

"Intelligence work," she said. "You were a spy?"

"Well," he said. He tried to smile, but his face felt so numb that he only managed to lift up one corner of his lip. "Sometimes. My job was to stake out the bars in town where the American GIs hung out. I was looking for foreign agents to try to recruit our guys to sell them military secrets."

"Did you catch any enemy agents?" she asked.

"Well. Some of these guys might have been spies. But they must of been off duty, because all I ever heard them ask our guys was if they wanted drugs or a blowjob."

"You're kidding."

"No. It was funny. I'd type out the conversations and submit my reports to my commanding officer. The people in my office, we'd take turns taking the parts of the soldiers or the Germans and act them out like plays. We had a good time. Anyways, doing that kind of work, the training you get, you learn to think on your feet. You find out how to find things out. So what I can find out for you, Miss Sheehan?"

"First of all," she said, "please don't call me Miss Sheehan. The last time I was called Miss Sheehan was by the nuns at Our Lady of the Assumption in Lynnfield. My name is Maureen. Second of all – "

He wished people wouldn't say "second of all." It sounded too much like "seconal." He didn't even know what seconal was, but just the sound of the word made his mouth water.

"Seconal," she said, "what I need is pretty simple, I guess. Well. Really not that simple. It's... fuck me."

"Relax," he said. "Take your time. Tell me a little about yourself first. You live in Saugus. Did you grow up there?"

"Yeah," she said. "I grew up in Saugus. I like Saugus. It's a nice town. It's home, you know?"

She finished her glass of wine and her cigarette, started fresh ones, and took a deep breath. "I went to business school in Boston and, well, you'll laugh, you've traveled, but Boston was, like, the big city for me. I always liked it. I still like it. But I like to go home. I traveled some myself, right after school. I had a little money saved. A friend and me went. She was a real pistol. I would of never of gone if hadn't of been for her. And it's a good thing I went. Because I figured out what I wanted to do with my. You know. Life. Paris is beautiful and Venice is beautiful, and the guys you meet traveling are great, it's a lot of fun for a couple of American girls. But you know what my favorite thing in Europe was? The little hotels. The really small ones with, like, eight rooms, where they give you breakfast. Even if it's just some bread and jam or something, and coffee, breakfast is a special occasion over there. I always loved breakfast. Since I was a kid. It's my favorite meal. I love to cook breakfast for people. I don't know why. So it came to me while I was over there. Get some money together, somehow, and buy a bed and breakfast place somewhere scenic. There are lots of them up in Maine. It's beautiful up there. Plants. Birds. Rocks and things. I love that shit. The bed and breakfasts there do good enough business that if things ever get slow you can hike and hang out with your dogs and just, you know, be at home. Some people would be bored, but not me. I'd be in pig heaven."

He waited, slowly sipping his drink, for her to continue. He hadn't shot that much dope, but he was like a sailor away from the ocean too long. He had lost his dope legs, and he felt loaded. He concentrated on keeping his right eye open and let the left one take a nap. Right eye open. Left eye shut. It was like a game. Dope Twister.

He listened to her warm, smoky voice. It was nice to hear someone talk who still had plans for their life. He had had plans once. Big plans. He was going to join the Army, get into the military police, learn police work. When he got out, he would get a job on a civilian force, work his way into the detective bureau. Then he could start accepting bribes, obstructing justice, tampering with evidence, trafficking in narcotics, soliciting prostitution, shit like that. He'd be flush with dope, guns, clothes, cars, and broads, and all legal, sort of. He'd be king. But things hadn't worked out the way he had planned. It was a little too late to become a cop now. Or a pharmacist.

"So," she was saying. "I got a place in Saugus, my parents gave me a car, and I started working for Pastorio Auto Leasing down on Route 1. This was about four years ago. I was just answering the phones when I started, but it was a small business and they were getting a slow start, so, because I knew computers, they let me help with the spreadsheets and get into the accounting, and do some work on the contracts for the car leases."

She smiled.

"Some of my friends from school told me they were taking advantage of me. I was doing all this extra work for a receptionist's paycheck, and I was never going to make enough to buy a bed and breakfast place that way. I thought maybe they were right. I did a lot of extra work for no extra money for a long time. But then business started picking up. They expanded the fleet. And they hired a new receptionist and made me office manager at twice the money I was making before. They did right by me. They always did right by me. Until now."

"Tell me about them," he said.

She sighed. "They're Saugus guys. Two brothers. Richie and Butchie. Big Italian family. They dress flashy and drive sportscars. Miatas. Mercedes two-doors. Red. Always red. They both like toys, real expensive ones, from that store, you know the one."

"Sharper Image," he said.

"That's it. Solar-powered shoe polishers. Computerized miniature putting greens, even though they don't either of them play golf. On the weekends they like to go into Boston and meet girls. Or they do guy shit. Ball games. I always felt comfortable with them. They treated me like one of the boys. They'd invite me to, like, their sister's wedding or a cookout at one of their houses. They'd bust my balls if I came with a date or they'd bust my balls if I came alone. We got along good. Everything was fine up until this past couple of months."

"What happened?"

"I wish I knew," she said. "They were always close before, but something happened a month, maybe six weeks ago. Something came between them. And it got worse just before Richie disappeared. The last week, they weren't even talking, except for Butchie yelling at Richie. Most of the time I couldn't tell what he was saying. But one day the door to the office was open and I heard him say, 'it's not up to you any more. Your way didn't work. Now we do it my way.' I don't know what he meant. But I didn't like the sound of that."

As he looked at her skin and watched her lips move, he felt himself falling into the rhythm of her story. He watched her with his good eye, but through years of habit he kept his other eye, the half of it that was open, wandering around the room. He saw two couples come in the front door and sit down at a table. He quickly put out his cigarette and fanned a couple of bills onto the bar.

"I'm sorry to interrupt you," he said quietly. "Someone just came in that I don't want to talk to right now. It, ah, has to do with, ah, a case that's pending. Let me take you somewhere else."

"Who is it?" she said, excited, starting to look around.

"Don't look," he said quickly, taking her by the arm. They walked to the door, Dave looking down and letting his hair fall over his face, and out into the street.

"Wow," she said. "That was exciting. Now come on, you have to tell me what that was about."

He smiled.

"Give me a minute," he said. "Let's walk up by the library."

"You really didn't want to talk to that guy, did you?" she asked.

"No," he said. "No, I didn't."

"This must have been some case."

"It was."

"Hey, come on," she said. "Don't clam up. You promised you'd tell me about it."

"Okay," he said. "Well. I'm not... you know. A philosopher. I take the world like I find it. I do my job. Nobody forces me. I try not to complain. Lately a lot of the work has been background checks. Girl meets a guy. She likes him. Things go good. Pretty soon they're engaged. But she wants to be sure he's not hiding something. She wants to be sure he's someone she can really trust. So she hires me to investigate him behind his back."

"You're fucking harsh!"

"You have no idea," he said. "Other times, I get to feel like I'm helping someone. Sometimes a chick will hire me. There's a guy bothering her, won't take no for an answer. You know. Stalking her. There's different ways to play it. One is to follow the guy around and videotape him stalking her, then show the guy the tape and threaten to send copies to the cops and his boss and his friends and his mother. Another way is to just go straight to the cops and try for a restraining order. It works sometimes."

"Sometimes?" Maureen asked.

He looked back up the sidewalk, then slowed down.

"Sometimes," he said. "If it doesn't, we look at our next set of options. They're all bad. You end up just waiting it out, mostly. Everybody lets it go. If not, I sometimes do a little short-term bodyguard work."

"Wow," she said. "What do the guys think about that?"

He smiled. "Drives 'em batshit. They're real tough going up against a girl, but against a guy, especially a guy with a gun, that we accidentally-on-purpose let them see, they piss their pants. Bunch of..."

"Pussies?" she said.

"I was going to say something polite," he said. "Like faggots."

"So what about this guy?" she asked.

They crossed Boylston, walked into the little park between the Public Library and Trinity Church, and sat on a bench. Some fucking idiot bum a few benches down kept saying "POO-hole! POO-hole!"

"Well," Dave said. "Sometimes we get a guy who thinks he's tough. Sometimes he is. That guy was. I was able to get him to see things my client's way, but I had to work for my money. I was just afraid he might want to continue our little discussion. Now that he's out of the hospital."

"Wow," she said. "Intense. So you saved her."

"Well," he said. "Sort of."

"What do you mean, sort of?" she asked.

"I mean sort of. That was her with him. He filed against me for assault. That was thrown out. I had a good paper trail. Her contract with me, the restraining order and pictures and voicemails saying he'd kill her and all types of shit. When that didn't work, she tried to file against me, too. For assaulting him."

"You're shitting me."

"You got no idea," he said. "Until you see it with your own eyes, you can't believe the shit they try to pull, shit I couldn't do without laughing. This dumb cunt – I'm sorry, my client, in her lawsuit, wanted me to compensate her financially for her loss of this guy's consortium. That's Latin for after I fucked him up, to keep him from fucking her up, he was unable to fuck her."

"What the fuck!" she said. "What was her lawyer, nuts?"

Dave smiled. "You tell me."

"What do you mean," she asked.

"Did he look nuts?" Dave asked.

Her eyes opened wide. "No! Him? He was her lawyer too?"

"And I used to think nothing could surprise me," he said.

"Man, you picked some kind of line of work," she said.

"Fucking tell me about it," he said.

Dave woke up. The teevee was on. There was an empty bottle of Bud on the nightstand. After a minute he remembered where he was. Back at the Midtown. To celebrate his success in his new career he had bought beer in bottles. Another couple of bottles stood unopened in a bucket of just about melted ice. He felt a little groggy but he wasn't hung over. The painkillers and tranquilizers and muscle relaxants and smack must have knocked him out before he could drink any more. Good thing. Drinking was bad for you.

He sat up in bed, opened a Bud, and took a sip. It was warm and a little flat, but delicious. He liked beer. He couldn't help it. He knew you weren't supposed to drink on top of narcotics. You'd OD and die. Or, even more embarrassing, you'd be too high to walk to the bathroom and you'd piss your pants.

The beer made him think of his father, who was actually named Bud. When Dave was little, back at the house in Lynn, they had a routine, a game. When Bud opened his first tallboy can of Bud after work, little Dave and his brothers would line up and each take a sip. By the time the Bud got back to Bud it was always empty. He'd just laugh and open another.

The old man was all right in many ways. In other ways he hadn't done so well. Nobody was perfect. Still, it was hard to forgive. He remembered lying in bed as a kid, listening to the arguments in his parents' room.

"I don't want him fighting," his mother said.

"I'm not talking about fighting," Bud said. "I'm talking about teaching him to defend himself. So he's not an easy target."

"Violence only leads to more violence," she said.

"No," he said, his voice getting louder. "Letting the other kids pick on him leads to them doing more violence. To him. A little violence from him would lead them to goddamn leave him alone."

"What if you teach him to fight and he starts picking fights himself, with weaker kids than him?" she said.

"There aren't any weaker kids than him!" the old man said. "And there's a difference between defending yourself and picking a fight. The kids he comes home crying that beat him up, they picked a fight. And if one day he made a punching bag out of them instead of the other way around, that would be him ending a fight they fucking picked. How can this not be clear to you?"

"Bullies want a fight," she said, calm, quiet. "They want him to fight back. When they see that he won't, they'll move on."

"Jesus Christ," he heard the old man say. "What the fuck could you possibly know about what a bully wants?"

"What would Martin Luther King do?" she asked. "What would Mohandas Ghandi do?"

"What would I do if you would once stick to the fucking subject?" he said. "We're not talking about Martin Luther Goddamn King or Mohandas Goddamn Ghandi or Ahab The Arab The Sheik Of The Burning Goddamn Sands. He's a real kid, in the real world, where real bullies beat him up. If he wants to let them, that's his choice. And if he wants me to teach him how to stand up for himself and throw a punch, that's his choice too. What right do you have to decide for him? What the fuck do you know about how he feels, about his pride? What do you know about trying to grow up to be a man?"

There was silence for a moment.

"Well?" Bud asked.

"I don't want him fighting."

Dave finished his beer and got up. "Fuck it," he said. There was no point thinking about the past. You could always find something there to feel bad about. It was funny, really. You were born being able to feel every bad feeling in the catalog, but to feel anything good you had to go to the goddamn fucking moon and back, you had to hustle like Superman, day after day in and day out, just to get a tiny little spoonful of dope into your arm. They gave you blood when you were born, like that was a favor, like that shit was any use except to shoot dope into. People talked about geniuses, about how Albert Einstein was supposed to be so smart. That fat fuck in his horrible old baggy sweater. The caveman who figured out how to grind up poppy petals and make a syringe out of wooly mammoth bones, that guy was a genius. If there was a god and he ever sent his son to save us, his son was the guy who invented dope, not Jesus Christ, that ratty haired scraggly bearded dress wearing faggot.

He looked around the room. Morning sunlight poured in through the windows. He liked this hotel. View of the fountains at the Christian Science Center. A real bed, with sheets on it. This was luxury.

He looked at himself in the mirror and laughed. The private detective routine he had run on that girl last night was brilliant. Academy Award material. It was just a mishmash of things he had heard and read and seen on teevee and made up out of thin air. The same shit that came out every time he opened his mouth. But it worked. People would believe anything if you said it like you meant it.

"You," he told his reflection, "are one of a kind, my man."

He fished his dope out from under the mattress, shot up, and sat for a while on the bed just looking out at the sunlight. Little rainbows glimmered in the mist rising off the water splashing in the fountains.

He put on a a light heather gray Brioni. Two button. Narrow lapel. His Jack Kennedy suit, he called it. It was a little warm for this weather, but shit. Any suit was a little warm for this weather.

He sat down at the desk and opened the bag from the office supply. He laid out a yellow legal pad, pens of different colors, different-colored highlighters, and sticky notes, all different colors and sizes. He took the cap off a pen. "Case #1," he wrote on a legal pad. "Richard Pastorio," he wrote. "Disappearance," he wrote. He underlined "Richard Pastorio." He underlined "Disappearance." He sat for a long time staring at the words. He lit a cigarette and opened another Bud.

"Fuck it," he said, and threw the pen down on the desk. He decided it was time for gun practice. He had never carried two guns before, and there were details to work out. He opened another bag, the one from the sporting goods store. He put on the shoulder holster and slid the Kid's magnum into it, under his right arm, where he could draw it with his left hand. The .45 he put into something called a 4-way holster that the Mossad had supposedly developed. He put it on the fourth way, at the small of his back, what they called an S.O.B. holster, the gun hanging sideways, barrel pointing left, the butt, of the gun, pointing up, in perfect position when he reached back with his right hand. He practiced drawing them together until he could do it without dropping either gun on the floor that much.

As he worked with the magnum he started to like it more. It didn't have the dignity, the history, of the .45, but it felt solid in his hand. The magnum caliber had been developed in the 70s for state troopers, to go through car doors. The .45 slug was a big fucker, but slow moving. Depending on the angle it hit, the .45 slug could bounce clean off a car door.

Now that all cops carried automatics you only ever saw a magnum on armored car guards. He always smiled when he saw them. The guards always, without fail, wore the gun low, halfway down their leg, like they had watched too many old cowboy movies.

He opened another beer and peeled the plastic off the videos he had bought for research purposes. He sat watching Bruce Willis, Chow-Yun Fat, and Antonio Banderas, studying two-handed shooting techniques. It looked like you could really take control of a situation with that much firepower, but reloading two guns on the fly looked like a motherfucker. He noticed that Chow-Yun Fat used something called a New York reload. In a firefight he pulled two guns out of the front of his belt and fired until both were empty. It was a movie, of course, so he had about fifty-seven bullets in each pistol. When he did finally run out, instead of dicking around with ejecting the empty clips and putting in new ones, he just dropped the first two guns on the ground, drew two more from the back of his belt, and started shooting again.

The movies were good, especially on his new teevee. The one that came with the hotel room was a cheap piece of shit, so he had pushed it into a corner and had the delivery men from the store wheel in some huge plasma extravaganza. It was great to be able to buy nice things without having to count every dollar, without worrying that there might not be enough left for drugs. He thought again about all the drugs and money he had now and just shook his head in disbelief. He made it a rule never to think about the future, but for now, at least, the good times were here. He hadn't even had to start using the cash yet. There seemed to be plenty of money on Cyrus' and the Kid's credit cards.

9

Dave crossed the Tobin Bridge and drove north on Route 1. He and Tori had sometimes driven this way up to Lynn to buy drugs, when everyone else was closed and they had no choice. Lynn, Lynn, city of sin, the old saying went. You never come out the way you went in. Ever since his family had left Lynn in the seventies to move into the city, he had only been back at night. The highway looked different during the day. His landmarks, the orange dinosaur that reared up over the miniature golf course, the huge neon cactus and the floodlit fiberglass cows in front of the Hilltop Steak House, the Leaning Tower of Pizza, and a sign for a roast beef joint that said simply FULL OF BULL, all looked small and hung over.

Dave drove into the parking lot of Pastorio Auto Leasing on Route 1 in Saugus. A salesman, a kid in a too tight suit, walked toward him as he got out of the car.

"Never mind, Billy," Butchie Pastorio called from the office door. Pastorio was solid, like an ex-college football player. He looked stern, like a coach whose team has lost. His jacket fit well. Athletic cut to give him enough room in the shoulders.

"You guys kill me," Pastorio said, shaking his head. "Look what you're driving. You might as well put the lights and the siren on top. Nobody drives a car like that but a plainclothes cop."

Dave looked back at the car, a blue Crown Victoria he had stolen that morning. Pastorio was right. It looked like a cop's car. Fuck. Maybe it was one.

"I'm sorry," Pastorio said. "What I mean to say is please come in, detective, I'll be happy to help you in any way I can."

Dave followed Butchie into the little office.

Butchie sat. Dave sat. Stacks of papers clipped together were piled neatly on the desk. A little toy red Mercedes convertible sat on top of one pile. Butchie put his elbows on the desk and his face in his hands for a minute, then sat back. Dave started to open his mouth, but Butchie held up his hand.

"I got the questions memorized," Butchie said. "And my story is the same. So let's run through it and we can both get back to work." He looked Dave up and down and said "You're Boston, right? 'Cause I met most of the plainclothes guys from Saugus when I leased them their cars."

"I'm Boston," Dave said.

Butchie picked up the toy Mercedes from the desk, spun its wheels with his finger, leaned back in his chair, and sighed.

"My brother Richie and me built this business together. Up until these past few months he worked his balls off, just like me. It's a good time for us right now. We're working more and more with the Saugus PD. We have a good relationship with the police. People in this country hear an Italian name, they automatically think ginzo, mobbed up, but we run a legitimate business.

"Anyways, couple of months ago, my brother started looking really sad all the time. And tired, like he wasn't sleeping. I asked him about it. We could talk. He was my brother. But he said it was nothing. Weeks, this went on. I asked him was it a girl, he said no, he wasn't going to bother with girls any more. I asked him what, was he a homo now, you know, just fucking with him, but he didn't even laugh. Another couple of weeks of this shit, I asked him what the fuck, was he sick, he said no, he wasn't sick. I asked him did he want to take a vacation, take the boat, we have a boat, a nice boat, I told him take the boat, take some time off, take a little cruise. No, he didn't want to take a cruise.

"Another couple of weeks, it's getting where I can't work with him in the office. He's not doing shit. He doesn't even pick up his phone. He's white as a fucking ghost. He looks like he's about to cry all the time. He won't eat, I order lunch in for him, it just sits there. He's got big fucking bags under his eyes. He's my brother, I love the fucking guy, and I'll pick up the slack for him if he's going through something, he doesn't even have to tell me what it is if he doesn't want to, he wants me to run the business, fine, I'll run the business, but I can't run the business with him sitting there looking like somebody just died, looking like he just fucking died himself.

"Finally one day I can't take the sad sack routine any more. I'm trying to lease cars to people and make some money. I say to our business manager, I say Maureen, help me out over here, take my brother home before I punch him in his fucking head! I'll deal with him tomorrow, but right now somebody around here has to do some fucking business!

"She takes him. I do some work and then I go home. It's late. I'm beat. I go to sleep. In the morning I make up my mind this is bullshit, he's gonna tell me what the fuck is the matter with him. If he needs a doctor, a psychiatrist, a fucking blow job, whatever he needs, he's going to have it if he likes it or not. I go by his place. I knock on his door. No answer. I break a window, I go in, I don't know what I think I'm going to find. But I don't find anything. Nothing. No Richie. He's gone."

911

Butchie and Dave came out of the office into the midday sunlight.

"Thank you for coming out, Detective Diamond," Pastorio said. "I'm sorry to see you waste your time like this. When my brother gets back to town, we'll get this sorted out."

Dave looked across the lot. A big bearish-looking guy with a stubbly reddish beard came toward them. He wore jeans and a bright orange Hawaiian shirt with dancing hula girls. A badge, cuffs, and a pistol hung from his belt.

"Jason!" Butchie called. The guy stopped in front of them. Butchie shook his hand. Jason looked at Dave. Dave kept his hands free at his sides.

"Jason, this is Detective Leo Diamond, from Boston. We've just been talking about our little mystery."

"Jason is with the Saugus Police," Butchie said. "Detectives' Bureau."

"Glad to meet you, brother," Jason said gruffly, not sounding too glad. "But I wasn't told this investigation had gone outside my jurisdiction."

Butchie smiled. "Jason is the Chief of Detectives."

Jason looked at Dave coldly. Butchie kept smiling.

Dave considered his options. They were all standing pretty close together. To get far enough away that neither of them could grab him and then get a gun clear and start shooting would take precious seconds. If Jason's reflexes were good, he might beat Dave to the draw. He might do what Dave would do in his place and take cover behind Butchie. If Butchie knew how close he was to taking a few slugs, maybe the smug motherfucker would stop smiling. Then too, of course, Butchie might be armed himself.

Dave breathed deeply, slowly, and relaxed his muscles, the ones that weren't already relaxed from drugs, from the top of his scalp and down his arms and legs to his fingers and toes. It was two guys against one. Bad odds. But what did that mean? Odds was just a word. Everything in life was fifty fifty. He'd live. Or he wouldn't.

"Jason, Detective Diamond has been very... respectful toward me. He hasn't said anything that might be considered... offensive to my ethnic heritage."

"Well, shit, Butchie," Jason said. "I'm glad as hell to hear that."

"Jason, Detective Diamond hasn't said, I did most of the talking, but if I'm not mistaken, his area of expertise in Boston is... organized crime?"

Jason looked from Dave to Butchie and back.

"There have been accusations made of foul play," Butchie continued, "of violence, and given the Italian names involved and the fact that it's a... family matter..."

"Got it," Jason said.

"But I think I've been able to put Detective Diamond's mind at ease," Butchie said. "And explain to him that this has been a misunderstanding. Now listen, I know how important networking is in any profession, so I'm going to let you fellas talk shop. Jason, let's you and I talk later."

Jason looked at him.

"You did want to talk?" Butchie asked.

"Oh. Well, shit, Butchie. I just wanted to test-drive that red Miata again."

Butchie laughed. "How many times will that be now, Jason?"

Butchie turned and walked back to his office.

"Well," Jason said. "Shit. Come on, I'll walk with you to your car."

They started across the lot.

"You know him well?" Dave asked.

"Butchie?" Jason said. "Well. Shit. I thought so. I mean, we've been looking into this disappearance thing with the brother, and yeah, until last week we thought, yeah, maybe he was involved."

"You said last week. What happened last week?"

"Last week," Jason said. "The week Richie called from Mexico. Didn't Butchie just get finished telling you?"

"That was his story, yeah. I just wondered if you'd had any contact with the Mexican police."

"The police? What are you, on drugs?"

They were almost to Dave's car when he stopped. Jason might wonder what a big-city detective was doing driving a hot-wired car.

"So run it down for me. What exactly happened?"

"Look," Jason said, stopping too, "I don't get it. I don't get who you are and I don't get what you want. What is the. You know. Focus of your investigation? Is it Butchie? He's what, a gangster, a wiseguy, and we didn't know about it? Or is this about me? You what, you drove up from Boston to bust my balls because you don't like the way I'm running this investigation? I'm a small-town hick fucking retard, is that it?"

Dave thought about saying that Saugus wasn't that small a town, but decided against it.

"Look," Jason said, "the story smelled a little fishy to us, too, all right? We're not that fucking stupid. The brother calls from some tropical island and says he's on vacation? Forever? He likes the margaritas, the senoritas, ay ay ay ay, he's the Frito fucking Bandito? But he'll only tell all this to Butchie? Okay, something's not right. Butchie tells us that he tells Richie we want to talk to him and Richie supposedly doesn't want to come back at all, but he agrees to fly up for a couple of days just to get this straightened out, then he's leaving again? Okay, something's fucked up. But we have an appointment with Richie at my office on Monday, and until he shows or he doesn't show, the investigation is on hold. All we've got is the girl, the office manager, calling my office every day, calling the fucking mayor. You know how it is. She makes a noise, we got to look into it. We're looking into it. So, in, like, a word, what the fuck? What's your interest in my case?"

"Listen," Dave said. "I'm sorry. I didn't mean to come on like a prick. Butchie's right about my specialty. My boss hears about your case, I don't even know how, and he gets a bug up his ass, like, what, our Italians are reaching the fucking Black Hand from the North End up Route 1 to your Italians out here? The fuck do I know. He sends me here to fly the flag. I come. I fly the flag. It's nothing. It's shit. I got no beef with you or your bullshit case. I'm out of it. I'll make a note in my report that you were instrumental in my investigation. I appreciate your talking with me."

"Well, fuck," Jason said. "Why didn't you say so?"

10-4

Dave opened the door to his room at the Midtown and reached for the light switch. A fist hit him hard in the stomach. He went down, gasping for air. The door slammed shut behind him. He heard a gun being cocked and felt the barrel pressed against his temple. A hand patted him down, pulling the magnum out of the shoulder holster, then the .45 from the 4-way. The lights came on. There were two of them. One sat relaxed in a chair by the window. The one who had hit him stood in the center of the room pointing a gun. He threw Dave's pistols onto the bed.

"Hello, Davey," said the one in the chair.

Dave took a few deep breaths and pulled himself up, sitting with his back against the door. He looked around the room. The mattress had been pulled off the box spring. They had gone through the closet and the dresser drawers and thrown clothes all over the floor. One of them had even kicked over the nice neat pile of pizza boxes he had made by the door. It was a good thing he had gotten a storage locker for the dope, the money, and the shotgun.

"Hello, Paulie," Dave said.

"Hello who, Davey?"

"Hello, Mr. Murphy."

"That's better, Davey."

Murphy was a tall man with watery grayish eyes, pale skin, and a gray crew cut. His face looked like it had been through a lot. A lot of windshields. It reminded Dave of the faces you saw in South Boston, old guys drinking pints of Bud in the morning in corner bars with Irish names where they didn't serve any Irish beers.

"If you don't mind my saying so, Mr. Murphy," Dave said, "that's a very nice suit you're wearing. Brooks Brothers?"

Murphy looked down at his suit. "Yeah," he said. "Brooks Brothers. What about it?"

"It's a good-looking suit," Dave said, "but with your coloring, the gray suit, the gray – I mean the silver – hair, you really need a splash of... something, to, you know, liven it up. I'd retire that blue tie, it's too wide anyway, and try a red foulard."

Murphy looked at his partner. Dave recognized the guy now. He and Maureen had seen him with Murphy at the bar in Copley. Murphy pointed to Dave with one of his shiny wingtips. "Hit him again," he said.

Dave turned into the kick and took most of it on his shoulder, but the toe in the ribs hurt. Fortunately Murphy's goon was wearing sneakers. In his jeans and jacket, a blue windbreaker with the Red Sox logo, he would blend in perfectly with the sports fans swarming into town from the suburbs and lining up for night games at Fenway Park. He had the powerful shoulders and arms of a boxer and moved like one. Dave guessed he had surprised a lot of guys with that kick, guys who thought they were in a fistfight.

"Davey," Murphy said. "I'm not a violent man. But Sean here is. Don't talk shit to me. We clear on this?"

Dave nodded.

"All right. Now Davey, I'd like to leave the past behind. We'll start fresh. With today. Do you know what today is, Davey?"

"Uh... Tuesday?"

Murphy looked at Sean. Sean brought up his fists, lowered his head, and took an ominous shuffling step toward Dave.

"All right, all right, all right," Dave said. "Today was the day I was supposed to check in with my probation officer."

"That's good, Davey. And did you check in with your probation officer?"

"I'm sorry, Mr. Murphy. I'm just starting a new job, and – "

"Davey," Murphy said. "Davey. Excuse me. Do you think I give a flying motherfuck what you were doing today? Do you think I give a rat's ass about what any of you junkie piece of shits do in your spare time? Well? Do you?"

"Uh, no?" Dave said.

"That's right, Davey. I don't. What do I care about, Davey? You know the answer to this one."

"Your fucking money, Mr. Murphy?"

"That's right, Davey. My fucking money. But that's not all I care about. I'm running a business here, Davey. You know about running a business. How does a business have to be run?"

"In a... businesslike way?"

"Very good, Davey. Now, tell me this. How do you think it looks when a probation officer sits behind his desk all day and nobody comes in to see him? They break their court-mandated appointments, which is supposed to have severe and immediate consequences, right under the noses of everyone in my fucking department, but none of them ever get violated? They never have a dirty urine? They all supposedly have jobs? They never get in any kind of trouble? And their probation officer has more money than a probation officer makes, so much that he's wearing Brooks Brothers and taking early retirement? What do you think that looks like, Davey? What business do you think that makes it look like I'm in?"

"Uh, solicitation of bribery? Felony falsification of documents? Lying under oath - "

"That's enough, Davey. Nobody likes a smartass. Now, if you can say everything I want to hear, why can't you do what I need you to do? Why can't you follow two simple rules? Why can't you give me my fucking money, and why can't you show up for your fucking office appointments? What is wrong with you that I have to explain this to you of all people, Davey, all the times you drove Tori to her appointments with me? Do you want to go to jail too, Davey?"

"No, Mr. Murphy."

"Well, then."

Dave took out his wallet and handed it to Sean. Sean handed it to Murphy. Murphy took out all the cash, threw the wallet back to Dave, and sat counting the bills. Dave admired the suit. Not his style, personally, but it did look good. He wondered if when

September came Murphy would continue with the college professor image, get a tweed blazer with brown suede elbow patches, maybe start smoking a pipe.

"Very nice, Davey. This will cover the paperwork for today's appointment, an additional charge for the pain and suffering you caused me by not showing up, and a little something to compensate Sean here for taking time out from his busy schedule to help, uh, facilitate our little meeting. Thank you, Davey."

"You're welcome, Mr. Murphy."

"Thank you, Davey," Sean said.

"You're welcome, Sean," Dave said.

He looked at Sean. Sean looked at Murphy. Murphy lit a cigarette.

Dave assessed the situation. When these jamokes finally decided to leave, he would have to get up so they could open the door. As he came up into a crouch, he could get the .25 clear of the ankle holster, jack a round into the chamber, put a couple in Sean, make a dive for the bed, grab the .45, take Murphy out, then come back and finish Sean off. It was risky. Sean still had his gun, a Glock, out and pointed vaguely at him. .25 was a pretty small caliber without much stopping power, even at this range. If he could get in a head shot, maybe two head shots, Sean would probably go down and stay down. But that left Murphy, who might be carrying or might not.

"There's, uh, one other thing, Davey," Murphy said. "This new job you said you started. What is it?"

"Private detective. Working a missing person case."

"Hmm. Private detective. I didn't see a license in your wallet."

"You know I lost my license for driving under the influence, Mr. Murphy."

Murphy laughed. Sean laughed.

"I meant your detective's license," Murphy said.

"My what?" Dave said.

They laughed again.

"You're a piece of work, Davey," Murphy said. "You'll go far. So. Private detective. That's why you're carrying not one but two unlicensed handguns?"

"You know I'm not good with paperwork, Mr. Murphy."

"I know that, Davey. So. You're not selling any dope?"

"No sir, Mr. Murphy. I'm just a customer now."

"I see. And where are you buying?"

"I go down to Blue Hill Ave and buy from the niggers, just like everybody else."

"Hmm. You haven't been by to talk to Cyrus?"

"Well, to tell you the truth, Mr. Murphy, I'm not accusing anybody of anything, but ever since Tori and me got popped, just by coincidence, right after we left Cyrus' place, I haven't felt like I want Cyrus to know anything about me or what I do, so no, I haven't been by."

"Then you don't know him and the Kid got topped a few days ago and robbed of all their stuff and their money?"

"Holy shit. What happened?"

"I just told you. They got greased. Somebody they knew. Shooter got close. Forensics says the wounds were all from two or three feet away. There was no powder on the Kid's hands, so it doesn't look like he got the chance to return fire, though we can't be sure because we can't find his gun. You can't miss the thing, it's an old Colt Python with these fruity-looking wood grips. You wouldn't of seen anyone selling something like that around the streets, would you of, Davey?"

Dave very carefully kept his eyes from turning toward the pistols Sean had thrown on the bed. He slowly started to bend his knees and pull his ankles toward him.

"No. No I haven't," Dave said. "Jesus. It looks like I got out of the dealing business just in time."

"Well, Davey," Murphy said, a smile on his face that didn't look friendly, "that's something I'd like to talk to you about. You see, Cyrus and I and the Kid and some friends in Narcotics, different detectives than the ones who rousted you and Tori, have been doing business out of that house for a long time, making real good money."

"Sure," Dave said. "Everybody knows that."

"What did you say, Davey?"

"I said no, Mr. Murphy, I had no idea."

"That's what I thought you said. Well, this incident unfortunately leaves our team short one sales manager and one security consultant. I thought the Kid would do a better job on security than he did, him being a former Boston police officer. We have Sean here in mind to take over for him."

"Is Sean a former police officer too?" Dave asked.

Murphy laughed. Sean laughed and held up his badge.

"I see," Dave said. "And who do you have in mind for Cyrus' job?"

"I was thinking of you, Davey."

"Me?"

"Am I, like, speaking Gaelic here or something, Seano?" Murphy asked.

"I understood you, Mr. Murphy," Sean said.

"You, Davey," Murphy repeated. "You know the business. The customers know you. With your military training, maybe you can help Sean set up a better security system than that dumb fucking lawn jockey Cyrus had. Now, as it happens, the Homicide detectives who are looking at the shootings are friends of our friends. They're people we can do business with. But everybody agrees that we should let things cool down for a while before we open for business again. You go ahead and dick around with your missing person for another two or three days. Try to stay out of the way of the real cops. And when you come in for your next office appointment, don't worry about bringing me my money. Consider it an advance on your salary. Just be ready to start your new job. You'll be helping a lot of people, Davey. You can really contribute to the greater good of. You know. Humanity."

Murphy stood up. Dave got up and leaned against the wall. Murphy started to cross the room. Dave's mind raced. Sean's gun was still out but pointing at the floor. If he would only put it away, Dave could acquaint them both with his policy that no one threatened him or pointed guns at him. Then the thought came to him that these clowns had partners, cops who knew him but who he didn't know. Cops they had probably told they were coming here. Cops who could easily be waiting downstairs, or even out in the hall. Another thought came to him as Murphy reached the door. He had checked that the .25 was loaded, but he hadn't test-fired it. There was no guarantee the fucking thing even worked.

"Davey," Murphy said, standing over him, "I have high hopes for you in this new job, and for Sean too. It's too bad he had to rough you up a little today, but that's business. Seriously, think long term, Davey. I think the two of you boys could be a great team. We could all be friends. We could make some good money. Think about it. But decide to do it, or I'll have Sean kill you."

Murphy walked out into the hall. Sean stood in the doorway. He slipped his gun into a holster on the back of his hip but kept his hand on the butt. His eyes flicked over at the bed. "Nice magnum, Davey," he whispered. "Nice grips." He smiled, stepped through the door, and pulled it shut behind him.

Dave got up and locked the door. He looked at the guns on the bed. All right. So he shouldn't have kept the Kid's magnum. He should probably throw away Cyrus' green suit, too.

.38

Dave turned off the highway onto the streets of Saugus. With no dinosaurs or leaning towers of pizza to guide him, he got lost. He drove around for a while, listening to the radio. The radio was like a day care center. There were a lot of women, girls, and babies.

American woman. Gold dust woman. You're every woman in the world. To me. Woman. Woman. Have you got cheating on your mind? She aches just like a woman, but she breaks just like a surfer girl. Brown-eyed girl. Young girl, get out of my mind. Girl. You'll be a woman. Soon. Baby. Baby. Don't get hooked on me. Baby. Baby. Where did our love go? Baby. Baby. You're having my baby. So walk like a man.

Dave changed the station. The car he had stolen was old, and you turned a knob instead of just pressing a button. A bunch of songs came on that were about dope. Double shot of my baby's love. Needles and pins. Horse with no name.

It crossed his mind that he had no idea what the people in the songs looked like. They were from a time before music videos. He had no idea, for example, what the chicks in the Bee Gees looked like.

He pulled up outside Maureen's apartment building. There was no one in the parking lot, but people in the apartments might look out their windows and see him shooting up. He pretended to be looking for something under the seat while he cut open a few bags and snorted them.

He rang Maureen's bell and she buzzed him in, then met him at her door.

"Wow," she said. "I like your suit. That color green is nice. And those buttons. Snazzy."

She wore a crimson-colored sweatshirt and sweatpants. The sweatshirt was zipped halfway down in front, showing a wife-beater stretched tight. She turned and hurried to the kitchen. He followed. She had pinned her hair up in back. Red strands had come loose, spilling down the back of her neck. The sweatpants' clingy fabric didn't show any panty lines.

Her condo was nice. He didn't see any of the frilly pink shit you usually saw in chicks' apartments.

"You're just in time," she said. "I've been practicing my technique."

She slid something that looked like a pancake out of a pan and onto a plate. She rolled it up, like an omelet, kind of, and sprinkled powdered sugar some type of liqueur on it. She put a few strawberries on the plate and handed it to him.

"Crepes a' la Sheehan," she said.

"Ooh la la," he said.

"Let's go in the living room," she said. "We'll dine informally."

They sat on the couch. She brought him silverware and a beer and sat down with a glass of wine and a crepe.

"This is really good," he said.

"Thanks," she said. "It's good to be doing something. Anything. I'm going nuts here. You know. Thinking about our case. Trying not to think about our case. I decided I had to got to do something, so I started cooking. These came out okay. The first few times I tried they ended up kind of leathery. I put them in a Tupperware. I give all my failures to my parents' dog when I go over there. The dog loves my cooking."

"Lucky dog," he said. "I used to laugh, you know, when I first went in the Army. The guys would complain about the food. The worst shit they gave us was better than what I grew up eating. My mom, you know, she did her best, but it was like we were stuck on a wheel – Hamburger Helper, Tuna Helper, then Shake and Bake Chicken, Shake and Bake Pork, Shake and Bake Helper, and those potatoes – "

"In the box?" she asked.

"From the flakes," he said. "That's the ones. And Minute Rice. And Rice-A-Fuckin'-Roni – "

"The San Francisco Treat!"

"Jesus fuck," he said.

They ate for a while.

"I don't know what I'm going to do," she said. "You know. With myself. Whatever way this thing with Richie turns out. I'm still going to have my life to live. I'm about at the end of the money I had saved. I'm not going to be able to buy a bed and breakfast any time soon, but maybe I could go to work at one of them. Cooking breakfast. It would be something. I need a change. I'm done with the car business at this point."

Dave nodded, leaning back on the couch. It occurred to him that it had been a long time since he had met a new woman he wasn't selling narcotics to. He had noticed before, and he noticed again, that Maureen Sheehan was a good-looking woman. With her pale, fine skin and the red hair and green eyes, his father would have said

"Her face is the map of Ireland." He was full of quaint old sayings like that. Of course, he also said things like "They all look alike in the dark," and "You don't have to look at the mantelpiece when you're poking the fire, and "If there's grass in the infield, play ball." He was a lot less quaint when his wife wasn't around.

As the finished his crepe, Dave thought about the fact that she hadn't mentioned a boyfriend yet. They usually brought that into the conversation as soon as there was a chance. He thought about the kind of boyfriend a girl like her would have. He would have lots of pairs of jeans, but only as many suits as he thought he needed. He would think it was okay to wear brown shoes with a gray suit. His shirts would be 50% cotton and 50% polyester. She would tell her friends he was "wicked nice."

"That was delicious," he said, putting his plate on the coffee table.

"Thank you, Leo," she said.

"This is great," he said. "I never get a chance to sit down any more and enjoy my food. I'm always. You know. Working. This job. I eat a lot of Burger King. My food groups are Alcohol, Tobacco, and Firearms."

He debated with himself whether to tell her that for breakfast he had eaten buffalo wings, but that he had been afraid to get the sauce on his clothes, so he had ended up taking them off and eating his wings in the nude. Probably the story could wait.

Maureen looked at him.

"So, uh –" she said. "I'm afraid to ask, but what happened to your face? You're all red."

"Tanning salon," he said.

"You're kidding," she said, laughing. "Where?"

"Newbury Street," he said. "Tanorama."

"Wow," she said. "I wouldn't expect you to go for something like that. You seem so... you know. Macho."

He shrugged. "I like the sun. But I've been working nights a lot. I didn't know if I was going to get to the beach at all this year, and the summers in Boston are what, three fucking weeks? I just got paid some money from uh, another case, and I figured what the fuck. It was my first time. I didn't realize the lamps they used were so bright. I guess I got a little burned."

"How far does it – I mean, did you take off all your clothes?" she asked.

"I wore a sock," he said.

"A sock?" she asked. "Why wouldn't you want to tan your foot?"

"I didn't wear it on my foot," he said. "This is a nice place you have. You don't have a cat."

"No. You're not a cat person," she said. "I can tell."

"How?" he asked.

"Uh, cat hair?" she answered. "On your legs? Of your suit? Jesus, what kind of detective are you?"

"I wonder sometimes," he said, and laughed. She laughed too. She had a sexy way of laughing. He liked it one bit.

"I'm sorry," Maureen said. "I shouldn't bust your balls."

"Get in line," he said.

"What, you're married?"

"Not exactly," he said.

"Divorced?" she asked. "What happened?"

"Oh, you know. Things. It was a long time ago. She moved. Away. Her career. I'm not sure what she's doing now. We haven't had a chance to talk."

"Why is that funny?" Maureen asked. "What's that smile for?"

"I don't know," he said. "I was just thinking that this is the first chance I've had to talk about it. About her. The... friends we used to see when we were together... "

"You don't see them anymore," she said, nodding. "That always happens."

"Yeah," he said, smiling uncomfortably. Telling the truth, even something close to it, was making him nervous. Lying was all right as long as you did it all the time, made it a way of life. If you started letting yourself forget, you could find yourself saying things to strange women like "Yes, I had to shoot them to death."

"I'm sorry," Maureen said. "I shouldn't pry. Tell me one more thing, though. That gun under your arm. Do you always carry it, or do you think you need it especially for this case?"

"It's best to be prepared," he said. "Life is. You know. Full of surprises."

"Do you like carrying it?" she asked.

"I... I guess I don't really think about it," he said. "I've made up my mind that I'm never going back to j– " He caught himself before he said "jail."

"Going back where?" she asked.

"Uh... going back to... just letting anybody fuck with me. It's. You know. A policy I have."

"Wow," she said. "I guess I better remember not to fuck with you."

"Good plan," he said.

"So, just one more question," she said. "I promise."

"What is it?" he asked.

"Well, you're always so dressed up. I'd think a detective could wear whatever he wanted. Especially in this heat, why wouldn't you just put on a pair of jeans and a t-shirt?"

"I don't wear jeans," he said.

"You what?"

"I don't wear jeans."

"What do you mean, you don't wear jeans? Everyone wears jeans. You're not telling me you don't own one pair of jeans?"

"I don't," he said. "I haven't since I was a kid."

"Now wait a minute. How do you live in America and not wear jeans? What's your story, anyways? How did you get to be such a… such a fancypants? Did you grow up rich or something?"

"No," he said. "I grew up in Lynn."

"That explains it," she said. "You grew up poor."

"Not at all. I lived in a nice enough part of town. My dad had a good job. I had five brothers, though, so the money he made had to go a long way. My clothes were hand-me-downs, or from yard sales. I didn't care. I didn't think about clothes then. I was a kid. Trying to get through school, that was the big thing I thought about. I didn't like to study. I could say I had attention depreciation disorder or something. But that's not really true. I just didn't feel like doing it, so I didn't do it."

"Didn't the teachers, like, ask you questions in class?"

"Sure," he said. "And I used to be terrified. But one day one of them asked me something I didn't know and I just opened my mouth and started talking. I had no idea what I was going to say. But I figured I had nothing to lose. It worked. I found out I could just run my mouth and throw in a little of this and a little of that and I could bullshit my way through just about anything. The teachers said I had the gift of gab. My dad said I was a bullshit artist."

"That's terrible."

"I didn't think so. I took it as a compliment. I liked being called an artist. I was good. I could fake just about anything. Everything but math. I was hopeless. It was pitiful. My dad had to sit and do flash cards with me, trying to teach me the multiplication tables, useless shit like that. Poor son of a bitch, in his wifebeater with a can of beer. Knickerbocker, he used to drink, or Narragansett. Trying to teach me math. Like teaching a monkey fucking brain surgery. Anyways, somehow, I don't know how, I finally made it to the end of eighth grade. My mom took me into Boston, to Jordan Mahsh, to buy a suit for my graduation. I looked at everything in the Young Men's department and I was about to pick out some gray or blue thing. Then I saw this… I can see it now. Like it was yesterday. I fell in love on the spot."

"What was it?"

He smiled. "It was a peach-colored polyester doubleknit leisure suit."

"No."

"Yes. They had dressed up a little mannequin with this orange suit and a navy blue Quiana polyester shirt with a long pointy collar."

She started to laugh. "That's so…"

"I know," he said. "I know. But I'll tell you. When I put on that hideous suit and that awful shirt and looked at myself in the mirror in the changing room, I felt like a totally different person. I felt like a million bucks. I felt like a man."

"You must have been so cute. It must have been painful."

"I didn't want to hear about cute," he said. "I felt suave. Didn't shave yet, never even kissed a girl before, but I swear, I felt like a real ladies' man."

Maureen laughed until her eyes glistened with tears. He chuckled, shaking his head. She put down her glass and wiped at her eyes with the backs of her hands.

"Oh my God!" she squealed.

"I know," he said. "But you know what's even more embarrassing?"

"There's more?"

"It gets better," he said. "Not only did I think I was a real bitch magnet. I felt like in that getup, everybody would respect me, like everybody would leave me alone and quit picking on me and fucking with me. In my Quiana shirt and my peach suit and a pair of Earth shoes, I felt like a real tough guy."

Maureen laughed until her face turned a purplish red. She pounded on her chest with her fist until she could breathe again.

"I can't believe you admit a thing like that."

"What the fuck," he said. "I was just a kid. The thing that's really funny is that after all these years, I still feel the same way when I put on a suit, so I guess the joke's on me."

"You're really something," she said. "One of a kind."

They sat for a while, Dave drinking his beer, Maureen's breathing slowly returning to normal.

"I hate to break up the party," she said. "I haven't had a good laugh in a long time. I needed it. I appreciate it. But you were going to bring me up to date. On our case."

"Yeah," he said. "Well, I went and saw Butchie Pastorio at the office. He's a hard guy to read. He tells a story well. It could be the truth or he could be full of shit. You know the kind of guy I mean."

"Believe me," she said. "I know. So what did he say?"

"He told me pretty much what you told me, up until the part where Richie left."

"What does he say happened after that?" she asked.

"After that he says the whole family was in a panic trying to find Richie. He says they were worried sick about him. He says Richie finally called from Mexico, said he went down there to get his head together or something, and he was fine. Butchie says he told you that, but – "

"That lying sack of shit!"

"But that you didn't believe that really happened and you got the police involved."

"Lot of fucking help they were. I should have known. Butchie is friends with all those cocksuckers. There's one real loser who used to come by on Saturday afternoon and 'test-drive' a red Miata. Until Monday morning. He didn't even bother to clean the beer cans and the used rubbers out of the back seat. He came here when I first called the cops in. I told him what happened. I told him I was afraid of Butchie. He told me I shouldn't be alone at a time like this. I said I was fine, I was going to spend some time with my parents. But that wasn't what he was talking about. Fucking pig."

Dave nodded. "Guy named Jason? Chief of Detectives?"

"Yeah," she said, surprised. "How did you know?"

"I met him," he said. "In fact, I was able to get a look at his file on this case."

"How did you do that?" she asked.

He shrugged. "Networking is important in any profession. So, according to the file, an angle that came up during the investigation was the possibility that Richie's disappearance might be connected to organized crime in some way. Now, was there ever anything that might have made you think-"

"No," she said.

"Not even a-"

"No," she said. She stood up and took his glass from his hand. She went out in the kitchen. He heard a cork against glass and a can opening. She came back with a fresh glass of wine for herself and a beer for him and sat down.

"I'm sorry," she said. "It's not your fault. That shit just bugs the fuck out of me. These asshole cops think because someone's family is Italian, because they're greaseballs, they must be in the Mafia. Give me a break. Assholes."

She lit a cigarette.

"Oh," she said suddenly. "Shit."

She laughed, embarrassed.

"I'm sorry. You're not, like... friends with a lot of cops, are you?"

"Me?" He smiled. "I wouldn't say that, no."

"Good," she said. "You know. Your line of work. I thought maybe-"

"Really," he said. "Don't worry about it."

They sipped their drinks.

"So," she said. "What else did it say in this file?"

"Well," he said, "the rest was stuff we know. Butchie's statement that he talked to Richie down in Mexico and that Richie agreed to fly back to town next week."

She shook her head.

"What?" he asked.

"Bullshit," she said. "It's bullshit. Butchie's stalling. He's playing for time. Why, I don't know. I don't know what he's trying to cover up. But the whole Mexico story is bullshit. It's a lie."

"Well," he said, "I have a few ideas about that. Let me run them by you," Dave said. He took a little notebook out of his inside jacket pocket and opened it. "Mexico would be a good place to run to if you've, I'm just saying, just for example, embezzled a bunch of money. Is it possible that something like that is going on and Butchie doesn't want to admit it?"

"Richie? Embezzle money from his own company?" she asked. "No. I can't see that happening."

"Okay," he said. "How about this? The heroin here is mostly Persian and Afghani, but the coke comes up from the South. Is it possible he was involved in anything like that? You and Butchie both told me they were expanding their fleet. Could they have maybe needed money to buy new cars and they weren't able to get a regular business loan and - "

"No. That much I know for sure. I did the books. They had plenty of money."

"Okay," he said. He turned a page in his notebook. There was nothing written in it, but it looked really professional. "Okay. Mexico is very popular with couples. Honeymoons. Romantic getaways. Is it possible, just for example–"

"No," she said flatly. "He wasn't seeing anyone."

He suddenly realized why she hadn't mentioned a boyfriend.

"Anyone," Dave said, "except you."

She looked at his face, then down at the carpet.

"Except me," she said quietly. She finished her glass of wine, then went to the kitchen and brought back the bottle. She filled her glass and lit a cigarette, looking like she might cry. She looked at him.

"Listen," she said. "Can I have a couple of those pills you keep taking?"

"They're, uh..." he said, "an, ah, antibiotic I'm taking for-"

"Oh, cut the shit," she said.

He gave her three and she took them.

"So," he said. "Can you tell me about it?"

"I guess," she said, sighing. "I always liked Richie. I always thought he was sweet and... I always really liked him. He was always nice to me. He treated me like..."

"One of the boys," Dave said.

"One of the boys," she said. "Which is not the way I wanted him to treat me. I tried to keep it, you know, light, with him, so he wouldn't see how I felt. I always liked him, but over the last few months, when he started to look so sad all the time, I just started thinking about him more and more and wondering what I could do to help him.

How I could make him happy. The night Butchie sent me to take him home I was really worried about him. He wasn't talking. I wasn't even sure if he knew I was there. Butchie said he would come over later to check on him, but I didn't want to leave him alone, so I waited. I cooked him some waffles, but he wouldn't eat them. So I ate them. They were good. Richie just went and laid down in bed. I wanted to keep an eye on him. I wanted to take care of him. So I got in bed with him."

She finished her cigarette and drank some more wine. She looked at him again. "Give me some more of those pills, okay?"

He gave her two more and she took them.

"So," she continued. "We just laid in bed for a while. I was nervous so I talked. I told him the same thing I told you, about the hotels in Europe and about my plan to get my own place in the mountains. After a while I ran out of things to say and I figured, you know, what the fuck, and I started kissing him. It was a lot of work to get him started, but once I did he seemed... fine... like there was nothing the matter with him at all. He seemed kind of distracted, but... that was... I don't know. Different. I guess I liked it. Later he fell asleep. I was still awake and I started to get nervous that Butchie would show up and be mad or something. I know it sounds stupid. We're all adults. But I felt weird. So I went back to my place to sleep. When I got into work in the morning Butchie was just coming from Richie's place saying he was gone."

"What do you think happened?" he asked.

"Fuck should I know," she said. "I don't trust Butchie. I just... I have a bad feeling. I just don't think Richie would have left without saying something to me. I don't believe it."

They sat for a while drinking their drinks, not saying anything. Her left eye drooped, then shut. The right one started to droop.

"These antibiotics of yours are pretty strong," she said.

He caught her wineglass as it fell out of her hand. Her eyes closed and her chin fell down on her chest. He stretched her out on the couch, found a blanket in the closet, and put it over her. She would be out for a while. He went into the kitchen to look for a spoon.

.380

Dave walked past the Prudential Building and wondered, like he always did, if they had told the architect to design the ugliest fucking building he possibly could. It looked like one of Maureen's waffles probably looked like when the dog was half finished eating it. Somebody should fly a plane into it and do the city a favor.

He crossed Boylston and went into The Pour House. It was a dump for college kids, but early in the day it was quiet and the buffalo wings were all right.

As he drank his coffee and waited for his wings, he was distracted by his hair, still a little wet from the shower. It was slick where it lay against the back of his neck. Wiping the hair away from his neck with his hand, he gave a little shudder at the slimy feeling. That morning he had actually stood for a few seconds looking at the blow dryer in the closet at the hotel. I will not, he had said to himself. A rule is a rule. Blow dryers are for broads and homos. No. I will not.

While he ate his wings, he made a list in his mind of his options. It was something the counselors in rehab liked you to do. You were supposed to realize that you could do all kinds of things with your life besides drugs. Christ, rehab was shit. The only thing it was good for was networking. You could meet a lot of new customers there.

So. Options. One. The private detective business. It was great. He could see now why detectives on teevee seemed so cool. Being a detective was the balls. You were your own man. Working for someone else was a loser's game, trying to get your foot in the door so they could slam it on you. Good luck staying on your toes and putting your best foot forward if your fucking foot was broken.

Then, two, there was the law. Working with Thomas sounded nuts, but there were angles to consider. If he was involved somehow in the law, maybe he could learn how to work out deals with judges and prosecutors in case he ever got arrested again. But that was ridiculous. Nobody was ever going to arrest him again and live to tell about it. Besides, there were sure to be problems working under Thomas.

Murphy's offer of the dealing franchise in Mattapan, three, was something to think about. The work was steady and easy enough to do. He'd have police sanction and his probation reports would always be excellent. He'd never be without drugs. He knew from Tori that when Cyrus had the job, if there were ever supply problems along the drug line, Murphy's cop friends could always get dope from the evidence room or some pharmaceutical shit, fentanyl or something, from one of their people at City Hospital. He and the Kid would tell you to your face they had nothing to sell you, but you never saw them in a cold sweat, shitting their pants, teeth chattering, trying to think who they could kill to get a spoonful of dope.

Three and a half, Murphy's guy Sean might not be such a hard-on once you got to know him. Obviously he had recognized the missing magnum, figured Dave had killed Cyrus and the Kid, and didn't care. To graduate from Murphy's legbreaker to a high-rolling drug dealer would be a step up. For Dave, it might not be so bad working with another guy for a change, talking guy talk. Maybe Sean's parents had sent him to Catholic school. The two of them could kill the time between deals talking Catholic shit, debating theological questions like what kind of hen pecked pussy whipped faggot was Joseph anyway, and did Jesus smoke.

Number four, another idea was some kind of combination. He could work with Thomas part-time. Deal drugs in Mattapan the rest of the time. But then he'd never have time then to develop his detective business. He'd have to stop taking cases, and his business cards weren't even ready yet.

The whole thing was getting too complicated. He had so many choices he felt cornered. People were always saying that when one door closes, another opens. Bullshit. When one door closes, buddy, you're fucking trapped.

Sometimes he thought the best job in the world was bottle nigger. You didn't even have to be black. You just went around with your shopping cart, picking bottles and cans out of the trash, then went to the recycling and got your money. Nobody told you what to do. Nobody shot at you in hallways. You never had to remember to pick up your dry cleaning or look at homo magazines like GQ to keep up with the styles.

He wiped buffalo sauce off his lips and finished his coffee. The waitress brought him the check. He counted the bills out of his wallet and gave her an big tip, just to get rid of the ones. He hated ones. You could be carrying around a wallet full of them and still have no money. He hated the white-haired faggot whose face was on them, Beethoven, or whatever his name was. Ones were almost as bad as change. Change, he really hated. If they ever put him in charge of money, coins would be outlawed. You could still collect them, if that made you happy. But if you were waiting in line to buy something, say, and some broad started digging in her purse looking for a penny, like you had all fucking day to wait behind her fat ass so she could pay with exact change, the cops would come and drag her away. They could do something goddamn useful. For a change.

The waitress thanked him and gave him his order of cold bacon in a Zip-Loc bag. He put the bag in his pocket. He walked up Boylston Street, traffic still heavy in the late morning. Didn't anybody have a goddamn job? At the library he sat on the steps. Judging by the ages of the kids skateboarding on the sidewalk and the fact that the liquor store across Boylston Street was closed, it was Sunday. He decided he would take the day off. Working with Tori, there had never been a day off. There were no holidays. In fact, holidays were their busiest time.

He thought about what to do with his day. He tried to think of somewhere he could go, something he could see. "Fuck me," he said after a few minutes. He couldn't think of a single thing. This part of the city was always full of tourists, but he couldn't figure out what they were looking at. The spot where some American guys shot some British guys two hundred years ago? A statue of some Revolutionary War guy, Abe Lincoln or something? What could be more boring that that?

Somewhere in the boxes of junk in his storage space there was a snow globe he had brought home from Heidelberg. In it, a tiny boat floated down a little Nekkar River, past the buildings of the old town. On a hill overlooking the town stood the castle, the Heidelberger Schloss. It made a nice little scene. He realized why you never saw snow globes of Boston. There was nothing to put in there. No Eiffel Tower. No London Bridge. You would never get anyone to buy a snow globe of the real Boston. It would have nothing in it but a Dunkin' Donuts, a rat, an old homeless bum, and maybe a bottle nigger.

He took out his phone. It would be a good day to see a familiar face, shoot some dope, and hang out with someone he knew. "Fuck me," he said, and put the phone back in his pocket. Everyone he knew was a hopeless runny-nosed dope fiend. They'd want to know where he had come up with all the dope. If they found out he was the one who had aced Cyrus and the Kid, there was no telling what they might do. They might rat him out and hope for a reward. They might try to steal his dope themselves. He knew better than anyone never to trust a junkie.

He made a list of everyone he knew who wasn't a drug addict. It was a short list. He thought about his brothers. He had their numbers around somewhere. None of them wanted him around their nice wives and kids. There was probably no use telling them that now that he had money and dope, he wouldn't have to steal their cars or their wives' jewelry to sell for money to buy dope. They wouldn't listen. They had had enough of him a long time since. He didn't blame them. From their point of view, they were right. He shrugged. Cost of doing business.

He could call his parents, of course. Yeah, he said, smiling to himself. Yeah, right.

What he really needed was a girlfriend. But she'd have to be a dope fiend. They were easy to meet. Narcotics Anonymous meetings, that was a good start. A normal girl, a nice girl like Maureen Sheehan, would never put up with his habit. But you couldn't very well put a profile on match.com, Junkie Seeks Normal Chick With Sense Of Humor About Dope. Or could you?

12

Maureen opened the door to her apartment.

"I'm glad you called," she said. "I need someone to taste this soufflé. I've been tasting it all day, and I can't tell any more if it's good or not."

"Glad to help," he said.

"Come sit in the living room," she said. "I'll get you a cup of coffee. You look like you're fighting to stay awake. Of course, you always look like that."

"Late night," he said. "Surveillance job."

She was wearing those red sweats again. He watched her as she went to the kitchen. Suddenly he needed to sit down. If she saw the front of his pants, she would know what he was thinking.

She brought coffee and they went into the living room. She sat on the couch next to him and pulled her legs up under her. He could see that she wasn't wearing anything under her sweatshirt. He realized that there was only one letter's difference between living room and loving room.

"So tell me a story," she said. "What was this job last night? Surveillance, you said."

"Yeah," he said. "It was one of those background checks I told you about. I'm going to need a career change if I keep having to do these fucking things. It's depressing.

"What happened?"

"Well. It was her parents' idea to have the guy checked out. She didn't want anything to do with it at first. But she had. You know. Doubts. About him. They were able to get her to go along with it."

"And? Jesus," she said, "it's like pulling teeth, getting you to tell a story."

"Sorry. Anyways, she gave me his social security number. With that, a lot of it is easy. You can find all kinds of shit online. And. You know. A few phone calls. So I found out he had a couple of arrests for possession. Heroin. Chickenshit amounts. Couple of bags. Personal use. He got detox. Rehab. Probation."

"He hadn't told her about this?"

"He hadn't mentioned it to her, no. The last arrest on his record was a year or so old, so it didn't mean he was necessarily still doing dope. I had to tail him all the way out to Roxbury to get him on video, buying a couple of bundles from some ni- uh, some African-Americans."

"You weren't going to say niggers, were you?"

"Can I have some more coffee?"

"Don't change the subject," she said. "It's a terrible thing to say. It's very racist."

"What do you mean?"

"Nigger? Hello? That's a racist thing to say."

"Why? It's just a word," he said. "It doesn't mean anything. It's. You know. A figure of speech."

"You don't hate black people?"

"Of course I don't," he said. "Why would I? Guy wants to be black, what business is it of mine? The fuck do I care? "

"Well. I never heard it put that way. But skip that n-word shit around me, all right?"

"Fine. You're the boss."

"Well? What happened next?"

"Oh, yeah. So, he buys dope from these spearchuckers - "

"Not funny," she said, trying not to laugh.

"From these jigaboos -"

"Stop it!"

"And goes home. That was last night."

"What now?"

"Well. I've got to call my client and let her know I've got something for her. She's not going to be happy. But her parents are. Those pricks'll be just as happy to prove her wrong as they are about saving her from a bad situation."

"That's sad. My folks have been so great with me. But this girl, she was, what, dating him seriously, and didn't know he was a drug addict?"

"Didn't know. He was a good guy, according to her. Job. Car. She said he was, you know. Wicked nice. A good boyfriend. What about you? What would you do? Would that be a dealbreaker for you?"

"Hmm," she said. "Normally, yeah, of course it would. But I don't know. If I didn't know when I met him. If I was already, you know, in love with the guy and I found out, I don't know. I might give him a chance. One chance."

"Fair enough."

"What about your girlfriend?" she said.

"Girlfriend?"

"The one you told me about," she said. "Your ex. Would she put up with something like that?"

"Uh… she might. She was very… "

"Easygoing?" she suggested.

"Yeah," he said. "You could say that."

"Well, what would you say? Come on," she said. "What is it, top secret? You're not a spy in the Army any more. Tell me about her. What was she like?"

"Well," he said. "She had black hair."

"And?"

"She had nice skin. Very sort of pale and fine. She was very proud of her complexion. The medicine cabinet at her place, you should have seen it, it was full of these bottles and jars of all different kinds of goop that were supposed to reduce the appearance of fine lines or replenish essential nutrients or restore a youthful glow. Every night before she went to bed she'd be in the bathroom putting some of this one under her eyes and some of that one on her neck. I'd ask what the fuck she was doing in there. I knew the answer, but it was funny hearing her say it. She'd say 'I'm cleansing, smoothing, polishing, purifying, illuminating, exfoliating, activating, eliminating, hydrating, oxygenating, rejuvenating, renewing, toning, firming, lifting and separating!'"

He took a sip of coffee.

"What's the matter?" he said.

"Nothing."

"You're blushing."

"Am not."

"Then why is your face all red?" he asked.

"All right, I'm blushing. Forget it. Just, if you use my bathroom, do me a favor. Don't look in the medicine cabinet. Anyways, never mind about me. Tell me about your girlfriend. I know she had black hair and nice skin. And?"

"And what?"

"Her personality," she said. "You know what I mean. What kind of person was she?"

"I don't know."

"What do you mean, you don't know? Tell me one thing about her."

He thought.

"She was a good businesswoman."

"Jesus Christ," Maureen said. "You make her sound like your boss or something. Did you. You know. Love each other?"

"I don't know."

"How can you not know something like that?"

"Well, she wasn't like other broads. Women, I mean." He took one of her cigarettes out of the pack on the table and lit it. "She wasn't." He blew smoke. "Sentimental. When we first got together, it just sort of. Happened. There was no real talk. I started spending a lot of time with her. One day she said why don't you just move in here, you're not even using your place. So I did. Time just. You know. Went by. We liked to look at the same things on teevee. We liked to go out for brunch. We'd get two orders of steak and eggs. She'd eat her eggs, I'd eat my steak, then we'd switch plates and I'd eat her steak and she'd eat my eggs. Her favorite part of the eggs was where they were brown from the juice, you know, from where they touched the steak. We got along. I liked being with her. I liked that there was no talk. I liked that there was never any of that shit about where are we going with this relationship. I hate that. How the fuck should I know where a relationship is going? What am I, a fucking fortune teller? What?"

"Nothing," she said.

"You're shaking your head."

She smiled. "It's just that you're such a guy. And, no offense, but I think your girlfriend was, too."

.22

Dave dreamed he was floating, cradled in the loving arms of the sea, gently carried out with the tide into the cool green depths of the ocean. It was a dream he dreamed when he was especially high. He also dreamed that he heard knocking, knocking, and clicking, clicking, like a door lock, and a large animal came into his room, like a bear or a walrus.

He opened his eyes. They would only open half, maybe a quarter of the way. He was sitting up in bed, leaning back against the headboard. His chin had fallen down to rest on his chest. He could see that he had at least managed to get the needle out of his arm before he lost consciousness. He hadn't rolled his sleeve up quite far enough and there was a spot of blood on his shirt that probably wouldn't come out. The tie wrapped around his bicep was looking pretty ragged, too. It was going to be time for a shopping safari soon.

He'd have to hit Filene's basement downtown. Whatever didn't sell in the swank store upstairs was marked way down and sent downstairs. For the price of a suit upstairs, you could get two in the Basement and still have enough for a bundle of dope. He realized that probably wasn't how everyone measured their savings, but for him it was a real incentive.

Slowly he raised his head and looked around the room. Jason was sitting in the chair by the window, drinking a Bud. Dave yanked out the magnum, pointed it at him, and pulled the trigger. The gun clicked uselessly.

"I unloaded it," Jason said calmly.

Dave dropped the magnum on the bed and started to reach around for the .45 in the 4-way. Jason smiled and held up a gun. It was Dave's .45.

"I took it off of youse," Jason said. "I didn't think you'd mind. You were pretty out of it when I first came in. Christ, I thought I was going to have to call nine one fuckin' one."

Dave slowly swung his legs off the bed and put his feet on the floor.

"No need to get up," Jason said, chuckling. "If you even think you can."

Dave looked at the carpet, breathing deeply and slowly. "What can I do for you?" he managed to say.

Jason laughed. "Jesus. You sound as fucked up as you look. You know, you're going to have a hard time enforcing the law if you can't walk or talk. But I guess you have your own ideas about enforcing the law, wouldn't you say, Detective Diamond?"

Dave rubbed his face and pushed his hair out of his eyes.

"What do you mean?" he asked.

"What do I mean?" Jason said. "Well, maybe you went to a different police academy than I did, but I'd say that your techniques differ from. You know. Traditional law enforcement procedure."

"What techniques?" Dave asked.

"What techniques," Jason said. "What techniques, he says. Well, there's car theft. While I was following you back from Saugus I called in your plates. That car was stolen this morning. You must have known that, because when you dumped it a few blocks from here, you wiped your prints off the wheel and the door handles with your tie. Maybe you can explain to me later, after you wake up a little, what a Boston police detective is doing driving around in a stolen car. I'm looking forward to that. Then there's possession of narcotics, of course. You know. Techniques like that."

"Ah," Dave said. "Those techniques."

"Yeah," Jason said. "There's also use of non-regulation weapons. I mean, look at this .45. What are you fighting here, World War Two? There's been some improvements in handgun technology in the last what... fifty years? You ever hear of a little something called a Glock 17? High-impact plastic frame? Weighs about a pound and a half? Holds fifteen rounds? You're carrying something that weighs twice as much and holds half the bullets. You gotta really think about joining the twentieth century, dude."

Jason drank some beer and smiled.

"Oh, and, uh, don't let me forget. There's serious mishandling of evidence," he said. "I got bored while you were drooling over there so I started watching some of your video collection. It looks like you've got surveillance videos of some drug dealers mixed in with your Bruce Willis movies. Doesn't that shit belong in, like, an evidence locker? Or is this some kind of conflict of interest, overlapping jurisdiction problem? You and your partner are on there buying drugs. What, were you on your own time and you got caught in somebody else's investigation? Where is your partner, anyway? Pretty girl. Nice rack. I wouldn't mind having her as a partner."

Dave put his face in his hands.

"And then there's the most serious charge," Jason said solemnly.

"What's that?" Dave asked.

"I talked to the clerk in the convenience store down the block, where you stopped in on your way back here after you dumped the car. You bought a lighter, razor blades, and a bag of cotton balls. The guy wasn't sure, but he thought he saw you take the spoon out of the cup of sugar by the coffee machine and put it in your jacket pocket."

Dave stared at him.

"Dude," Jason said. "That's shoplifting."

Jason guffawed and finished his beer, then went, laughing, over to the refrigerator and got another for himself and one for Dave.

"Shoplifting," he repeated. "Very serious offense."

Jason sat back down in the chair.

"But seriously. I'm not going to roust you for that. I'm not going to roust you at all. The way I see it, what you do on your own time is your business. I mean, working organized crime the way you do, it's got to be stressful. You're looking at some pretty bad guys. Maybe making them real mad. You've got to expect they're looking back at you. You need to get an armful to keep your nerves steady, hey, it's not for me to put you down. Other guys, they might not see it that way. They'd look at you, they'd see a guy out of control, a guy who's a danger to himself and to his department. A guy whose conduct should be brought to the attention of Internal Affairs. A guy who ought to be prosecuted like a common criminal, maybe do some time."

Dave opened his beer and drank.

"Me?" Jason said. "That's not what I see. What do I see, you might ask."

"Uh, what do you see?" Dave asked.

"I see," Jason said "my new partner."

"Partner," Dave said.

"Partner. Come on, don't look at me like I got three fucking heads. We could be a team. We see things the same. We have the same. You know. Philosophy of justice. You're out there putting your life on the line every day, trying to put these serious gangsters out of business. Guys we only read about in the paper out here, outside the city. You're risking your life to, you know, make the world a better place, all that shit. So you steal some cars, maybe you like to steal cars, I know guys with weirder habits than that. So you shoot some dope. Technically, these would be considered wrong things to do. But come on. We're all men here. What's the wrong you do compared to the good you're doing for, you know. Society?"

"You've got a point," Dave said.

"Fuckin' A I do," Jason said. "It's the same with me. Saugus is a tough town. You guys from Boston may laugh, but we got problems here too. I pull a guy over for speeding, how do I know, maybe he's going to come up with a gun and shoot me. You want stress, you pull a guy over and walk up to his car, not knowing if you're going to live through it or not. So he checks out all right, I let him off with a warning. Maybe while I'm looking at his license I take the money from his wallet. Big deal. He shouldn't have been speeding."

"Fair's fair," Dave said.

"That's how I see it," Jason said. "Another time maybe I arrest a coke dealer, and I take his stuff and snort it myself. Maybe that'll teach him we got zero tolerance for drugs in this town. I mean, come on. You know what I mean. Work with me here. Tell me you know what I mean."

"I'm with you so far," Dave said. "But help me. What is it you think I can do for you?"

"Partner!" Jason said. "Now you're talking! I knew we could make a deal. What you can do for me is, you can set up a special detail to investigate organized crime in Saugus. Run it by your boss and sell him on the idea. Let me work here and report in to you in Boston. I can bring a lot to the table. And I'm willing to let you have the credit. I don't give a shit about that. But I want a promise."

"Uh... that what?" Dave asked.

Jason smiled. "That you'll get me transferred to Boston, attached to your division permanently, partnered up with you. Like Butch and Sundance, we'll be. Like Thelma and Louise. I'm in high school out here and I want to graduate. I want to move into town. Into the big time. I mean, did you look around you when you were out there? Have you ever tried to buy decent coke in Saugus? Have you seen what the whores look like out there? Give me a break. I mean, what kind of standard of living can a guy have under those conditions? I'm not looking for a free ride. I can bust my ass when I decide to. I'll work like a nigger for you. Tell me we're on the same, you know, page, here. Tell me you hear what I'm saying."

"I hear you," Dave said. He nodded slowly. "All right. I'll do it."

"Man, that's great!" Jason said.

"Yeah, yeah, yeah," Dave said. "But you've got to work with me. You may have to be patient if it doesn't happen as fast as you want. The guys I work with think of themselves as an elite group. It's going to be tough convincing them to work with someone who doesn't have..."

"Any class?" Jason said.

"Any experience in a big-city organized crime unit," Dave said. "But if you've got the kind of information you're talking about, I'm pretty sure I can push this through. In the meanwhile, I'm going to have to ask you to keep this quiet. Confidentiality is key here."

"I got it, partner," Jason said.

"All right. Now, does anyone, anyone at all, know you're here?"

"No one," Jason said. "Not a soul. I'm undercover. I'm infuckingvisible. I'm the Invisible Man. You won't be sorry about this," Jason said.

"No," Dave said, smiling. "No, no I don't think I will. Now hand me that .45, will you? Partner?"

16

"I'm stoked about this," Jason said as they stepped out into the hall. Dave locked the door behind them and settled his reloaded guns back in their holsters.

"You're sure you can make it happen?" Jason said.

"Trust me," Dave said. "Now let's go get a drink."

"10-4, partner," Jason said.

The stairwell door at the other end of the hall opened. Murphy's goon Sean stepped out into the hall. Murphy stepped out into the hall. Then Tori stepped out into the hall. The three of them looked at Dave and at Jason. Dave and Jason looked at them.

Sean went for his gun first. Then everyone started to move. Tori jumped like a grasshopper back through the door into the stairwell. Dave drew both of his guns like he had practiced. The .45 caught on his jacket and clattered to the floor, but he kept his grip on the magnum with his left hand. Bullets ripped through the air around him. Plaster exploded from the walls and stuck in his hair. As he fired the magnum he knelt and picked up the .45 from the floor and started firing them both.

Next to him Jason was lying flat on the floor. Dave thought at first that he was dead, but he was firing slowly and methodically from the prone position. First Murphy and then Sean fell over like bowling pins at the other end of the hall. Jason jumped up and ran toward them. Sean was still alive, coughing, spitting blood, trying to reach his Glock where it had fallen on the carpet. He had just touched the grip when Jason shot him through the back of his head. Jason made sure Murphy was dead, by shooting him, again, then looked through the little window in the stairwell door. Tori had gone. He ran back to where Dave was kneeling.

"You all right, Sundance?" Jason asked. "You hit?"

"No, no, I'm fine," Dave said. They could hear screams and shouts behind the doors of the other rooms, but no one dared to come out.

"So," Jason said, ejecting the clip from his Glock and slipping in a fresh one he pulled from his belt. "The fuck was that all about? Who were they? And dude... wasn't that your partner?"

"Yeah," Dave said. "Yeah, it was."

Dave stood up and slipped the magnum back into the shoulder holster.

"And?" Jason said. "The guys?"

"The guys..." Dave said. "Fuck. This isn't good."

Dave started talking fast. "The guys are organized crime associates from Boston. They supply dope to the dealers that you saw me and my partner buying from in that surveillance video. Only she's not really my partner. She's not a cop. She's a junkie, someone I busted last year, she's my snitch now. Those guys had some dope and money stolen off them earlier this week. Maybe... shit. I don't know, maybe she told them I did it. Maybe she told them I'm a cop. She must have known they'd kill me. With me dead, there'd be no chance I might turn her in someday when maybe I didn't need her any more. I'd be no threat to her."

Jason looked happy. "Excellent. We shot some real bad motherfuckers."

"Well, yeah," Dave said. "But I'm sorry, Jason. The reason I'm, you know, familiar with them is that, besides their jobs in crime, they were also employees of the Commonwealth of Massachusetts. You just killed a probation officer and a Boston Police Department patrolman."

The pink glow drained out of Jason's face and he slowly went green.

"Great. That's fucking great," he said, and leaned against the wall.

"Listen," Dave said. "I'm counting on you to keep it together here, partner. You keep it simple. You state that it was self-defense. You've never seen these guys before. They didn't identify themselves as police officers. Keep it simple, keep it clean, and we'll get through this."

Dave looked down at the carpet.

"Oh, shit," he said.

"Christ!" Jason said. "What now?"

"Jason, your shells. 9 millimeter?"

".40," Jason said.

"Jason, stay with me here. They're going to find my shell casings in with yours and they're not going to match. Say that... say that... give me a minute..."

Jason looked at the floor. The casings were everywhere, like popcorn in a movie theater.

"Jesus motherfuck!" Jason said.

"I've got it," Dave said. "Listen to me, Jason. Say..." he continued, picking up speed, "say you were with a girl. You picked her up in the street. She said she had a room here. Admit she was a whore. Act embarrassed about it. If you say you met her in a bar they'll go there and ask around and no one will say they saw you and back up your story. Say you met her in the street. Say... say you think those two were after the girl. Say that the girl pulled a .45, a compact .45, say it was gold-plated, with... with ivory handle grips, a real pimp gun. Lay it on thick, you got nothing to lose. In fact, say she pulled two guns, the mini-.45 and a little bulldog magnum. That'll explain my magnum slugs in the wall back there. Stay with me here, partner. You can do this. You're going to get one chance and you've got to be ready. Jason, I feel like I know you. I feel like I can trust you. That's why I was willing to work with you in the first place. You can be a great undercover man, but you've got to start now, tonight. You've got to tell a big lie and stand by every detail until the bitter end. But you can't think of it as a lie. If you make yourself believe the lie, then it's not a lie. You're not lying. You're telling... what are you telling, Jason?"

A tiny light of hope showed in Jason's eyes. "The truth?"

"Right answer, Jason," Dave said. "Now listen. Be ready with your description of the girl. They'll want you to sit down with a sketch artist. You've got to make a picture in your mind and stick to it. You were ready to pay to fuck her, so they'll expect that you got a pretty good look at her. Say she looked like..."

Dave looked down the hall toward the stairwell door.

Jason looked at the door, then back at Dave. "Man," he said. "You're fucking cold."

"No," Dave said. "No, don't say it was her. Say she looked like... Madonna. Say that's why you picked her up."

"You sure about this?" Jason asked. "I mean, maybe we should give them your partner. I mean your informant. I mean, am I wrong, or did she just show up with two guys and try to kill you? If we get a description of her out there, say she's armed and dangerous... maybe some trigger-happy street cop will solve your problem for you. I mean, I don't know the score, I'm just guessing, but it looks to me like someone's going to get hurt here and it's gonna be her or it's gonna be you. Am I right or am I right? What are you gonna do about her?"

"Don't rush me," Dave said. "I'll think of something."

They could hear the sirens coming from a few blocks away.

"Jason, listen. I have to go. I can't be seen here. I call attention to myself like this, I'm dead."

"So go," Jason said. "I got it under control here. She looked just like Madonna."

"You're classic, Jason," Dave said, sliding the .45 back in the 4-way and smoothing his jacket over it. "You're once, twice, three times a lady. Jason, I owe you. I owe you for what you're doing here, buddy. Partner."

"Yeah, yeah. I know," Jason said, "Get out of here and let me work." He leaned on the wall and started making hacking sounds like he was about to throw up.

10

Dave pulled in to the parking lot of the Howard Johnson's in the Fenway. After the shootout at the Midtown he had moved in. It was his first time staying there. As hotels went, it was all right. He didn't like the fact that people called it the HoJo. It sounded too much like homo. But fuck it. He had worse problems.

He sat in the car, watching the traffic lights change on Boylston Street, thinking about the suits he'd had to leave in his room at the Midtown. He thought about the guys you saw on the news after a hurricane in Florida, standing on the spot where their houses used to be. That was how he felt. He'd been ready for another year in Boston, prepared, with suits for every kind of weather, the different thicknesses of material for the changing seasons. He thought about the way the fabrics felt in his hand. Wool. Linen. Silk. The way the patterns in each different weave looked, the jackets hanging next to each other in the closet, like jewels in a treasure chest. Windowpane plaid. Harris Tweed. Herringbone. Houndstooth.

He thought of every possible way he might be able to go back and rescue them. But the cops would have the Midtown staked out, waiting for him, even if they bought Jason's story about the girl with the guns. They had lost two of their own, and they would want to question the shit out of everyone, especially the guy whose door the shooting had happened in front of. He might be able to bullshit them that he hadn't been home, that he didn't know anything about any shooting. But it was too big a risk. If they figured out who he was, it was all over. Even if he shot the first two, there would be more backing them up. He would need an assault rifle for an operation like that. And a car big enough to fit all his suits. Once the shooting started, the desk clerk would probably be on the floor, crying like a girl. Who would call a cab for him?

A terrible thought came to him suddenly. The desk clerk had probably described him to the cops. He could feel himself starting to panic, thinking about a sketch artist, the picture distributed to all the cops on the street. Then he had a worse thought. Maybe they had sent the picture to all the hotels, too. He took a couple of tranquilizers and painkillers from his pocket and swallowed them, but his mouth was dry and the pills stuck in his throat. He took a can of beer from under the seat, opened it, and gulped it down. The pills went down, but his throat still felt dry.

He took a deep breath and relaxed his shoulders. He reminded himself that it was ridiculous, pointless, to worry. What was going to happen was going to happen. Worrying was a poison that would eat your life, and didn't change anything anyway. Worrying was a game for old ladies. Worrying was for his mother. Fuck her. Fuck her sideways.

He walked past the desk, hands loose by his sides, ready, just in case. No one said anything to him. No cops jumped out from behind the ferns in the lobby. He smiled. He had forgotten for a minute what life was. There were no rules. You could do whatever you wanted. No one noticed, and if they did, they didn't give a fuck and a half.

Dave opened the door to his room. He smelled coffee. There were two styrofoam cups on the night stand by the bed, one full, one empty, and two empty beer cans. Steam was coming out of the bathroom door. He could hear the shower running.

Quietly he shut the door behind him and pulled out the magnum. He stood where he was and waited.

The shower stopped running. He pointed the magnum at the bathroom door. After a minute a girl came out, naked, thin but with a nice shape, drying her blonde hair with a towel.

"Hi, honey," she said.

"Jesus fuck, Tori," he said. "What the fuck?"

"Uh, honey?" she said. "Do you mind? Not pointing that at me? You can see I don't have a gun."

He put the magnum back in the shoulder holster and sat on the bed.

"Thank you, honey," she said. She threw the towel back into the bathroom, got two beers from a 30-pack on the floor, gave him one, and kissed him. They opened their beers and drank. She reached into a bag from the Levi's store and started putting on a new pair of jeans.

"Tori," he said. "Your jeans. They're... blue."

"I know," she said, laughing. "Aren't they awful? I figured I better change my image. Ditch the black clothes and the black hair. You like my new t-shirt?" she asked, pulling it out of the bag.

"It's so... white," he said.

"Change can be good," she said. "So. You haven't told me if you like me as a blonde."

"Very nice," he said. "You look good. You look... just like Madonna."

"Thank you, honey," she said.

"Tori, how did you get in here?"

She laughed, pulling on the t-shirt. "Maid. Told her I was your wife. Left my key. Didn't want to wake you. I had a couple of cups of coffee with me from the store across the street. She believed it. Let me right in."

"But how did you know to look for me here?"

She looked at him. "David," she said. "You love hotels. You were living at the Midtown when we met under the name King, because you said living in hotels made you feel like a king. I called a few places and asked if they had a Mr. King registered. I should be a detective, huh? Oh, I forgot. Murphy and Sean told me. Detective is your new job."

"Funny you should mention that, Tori," he said. "I never knew you were such great friends with those guys."

"Oh relax, David," she said. "It's not like it looked. I was trying to work some kind of deal to get my charges dropped. Murphy said he'd help me. He gave me a few hundred bucks and some dope to get me started. He wanted me to get back out on the street and see what I could find out about some dope and some money he got stolen off him. I don't know if you heard about it. Cyrus and the Kid are dead."

Dave nodded. "I saw it on teevee."

"Then they told me you were going to be working for them, at the house, and I thought maybe I could work there with you, that you and me could be partners again. I didn't know anybody was going to start shooting everybody."

"Listen," he said, finishing his beer. "Forget it. You did what you had to do. I'm just glad we got you out of jail."

"What do you mean, we?" she asked, handing him another beer.

"Me and... uh, how did you get out jail, Tori?"

"Murphy and Sean got me out," she said, tucking in her t-shirt. "They couldn't do anything officially, being, you know, in the cop industry themselves, so they went through an agency and put up my bond in cash. That's what they told me, anyway, when they came and got me."

"What about your mother?"

"What about her?"

"Never mind," he said. "What about your charges? You still have to go to trial?"

"Well," she said, smiling. "They're expecting me. But now that those guys can't help me I think I better just leave town."

"That's good," he said. "I mean, you know. You don't want to go to jail. When are you leaving?"

She stopped smiling. "As soon as you give me my half. Partner."

"Half?" he said.

"Half the money," she said. "And all the dope."

Fast, she stabbed her hand into the Levi's bag and came up with a snubnose Smith and Wesson .38, a Detective's Special. It was a good gun for people who weren't used to guns. Not powerful, but simple to operate. She stuck it in his face, pressing the barrel in the middle of his forehead.

"Don't insult me," she said quietly. "Don't try to tell me you didn't kill Cyrus and the Kid. Murphy believed you, that you had nothing to do with it. He didn't think you had the balls. He had already been to see you at the Midtown when they bailed me out. He told me the shit you said. This private dick bullshit. That was my first clue.

Like you would ever do anything with your life but chase after dope – unless maybe you already had dope."

"Tori, I- "

"Shut up," she said, poking him with the gun. "Murphy said he could tell you were strung back out again when they saw you at the hotel. He said you told him you were buying from the niggers. Well, honey, I know those niggers. Those niggers are my friends. And those niggers told me they never sold you any dope or even saw you since the last time we went down to Blue Hill Ave together."

"Come on, Tori. We all look alike to them."

"Funny," she said. "Very funny. I'll tell you the truth, David. I don't give a fuck who you killed. Those guys were shit. They deserved it. Fuck 'em. But you had money. And you were going to let me fucking rot in jail. If Murphy hadn't of bailed me out I'd of gone to trial and straight to fucking state fucking prison. That I can't forgive." She pulled back the hammer on the revolver.

"Tori."

"David?"

"Tori."

"I'm listening, David. But make it quick, motherfucker."

"First of all," he said. "You're too close. You get this close, a guy, if he's fast, can knock the gun out of your hand before you can pull the trigger, or at least before the hammer comes down. And if you do shoot me in the face at this range, my brains, what there are of them, are gonna splatter all over your nice new white t-shirt. Try explaining that to the cops. Seconal, you're right. Congratulations. They fucked with me. I killed them. I took their money and their dope. You call me a motherfucker, that's fine, but you want to talk about mothers, and about fuckers, the first thing I did when I got the money off them was I gave your mother a stack of cash to bail you out and send you on your way out of town. If she didn't do her part, it was my mistake, trusting her with that much scratch, but like I told her, you were always square with me and I wanted to be square with you."

"You're lying," she said. Her voice was cold.

"Ask her," he said. "Ask her to look you in the face and tell you I didn't give her an envelope full of money. Come on. Let's go over there now."

She stared at him. He peered at her around the .38. Anger, confusion, disbelief, then more anger and confusion played out across her face.

"You've got balls," she said. "Saying shit like that to me. About my mother. About Cyrus. You think you're such a great liar. You're not. I can always tell when you're lying."

She kept glaring at him. He took a quick look at the gun, hoping that by some chance he might be able to see light through the chambers in the cylinder. It was no dice. They were all full of bullets.

The gun started to shake. They did that when you held them out too long without firing them and your arm muscles tightened up. Dave wondered if maybe he should say something more. He couldn't think of anything. He figured it would be just his luck to get killed for telling the truth.

Tori breathed in. The gun stopped shaking. Then she let out her breath very slowly, just like you were supposed to when you pulled the trigger, so you didn't jerk the gun and miss your target. She slowly shook her head, then took the gun away from his face and let her arm drop to her side.

"That thing is heavier than it looks," she said calmly, looking down at the gun. She touched his forehead where the barrel had been.

"I'm sorry, honey," she said. "It's been a tough couple of days. I don't know what to believe."

She sat down on the bed next to him and took his hand. "I really am sorry. I should of known you'd do your best for me. About my mother... I can't believe it. I mean, I believe you, but I can't believe it. My own mother. That fucking slit."

She put the gun down on the bed, picked up her beer and finished it.

"So," she said. "What happened? At Cyrus' place?"

"Christ," he said. "I need a beer for this."

"I'll get it," she said. She stood up and reached into the case of beer for two more cans. Dave looked at the .38 on the bed. He looked up at the back of her head. He looked back down at the gun. Tori turned with the cans of beer in her hands. She saw his face, looked down at the gun, and stood still. He looked up.

"Where did you get it?" he asked.

"Murphy," she said. "He said if I found his dope to kill whoever had it. He said there'd be a cash bonus if I did. He said if it helped get the word out not to fuck with his operation, it would be worth it to him."

He looked down at the gun. "Makes sense," he said.

He looked up at her.

"He was really going to trust you to bring his shit back to him?" he asked.

"I don't know," she said. "He couldn't of thought I'd of brought much, but some of his dope back would of had to of been better than none."

"Hmm," he said. He put his hand out. She handed him a beer. He opened it and drank. She opened hers, drank, and sat back down on the bed, between him and the gun, he noticed.

"So," he said. "While I'm in rehab I have Thomas check up on you. You're still in jail. I get out of rehab. I go to see Cyrus. I think maybe I can get him to front me some money to get you out, or some dope to sell for money to get you out. I'm not, you know, holding my breath, but I think maybe he'll do it. For old times' sake."

"What did he say?" she asked.

"I didn't get to ask him," he said. "As soon as I get in the door the Kid starts pointing his magnum at me, and Cyrus is waving a pistol-grip shotgun around. They take my .45 and make me kneel on the floor. Cyrus starts talking all kinds of crazy shit about how I'm working with the cops, how I sold you to them and now I'm there to get evidence against him and the Kid. They want to know who my contact is, like I'm fucking James Bond. I says to him what the fuck, Cyrus, don't look at me, you're the one getting dope from the cops. He says how did you know that? I says Tori told me. The Kid says damn, Cyrus, I told you we ought to of capped that loudmouth skanky bitch!"

"What?" Tori said. "That little faggot called me skanky?"

"I would of stood up for you," Dave said. "But I was. You know. Kneeling."

"What did Cyrus say?" she asked.

"He says forget about that now, let's get back to business. He tells the Kid to pat me down for a wire. So what does the fucking idiot Kid do? He's got his gun in one hand and mine in the other. He sticks my .45 in the front of his pants and comes over to frisk me. I'm kneeling. I've got my hands behind my head. My hand is maybe a foot away from my fucking gun. I grab the magnum and push it away, so he doesn't hit me if he gets a shot off. I grab my .45 out of his belt. I shoot the Kid in the face. I shoot Cyrus in the chest."

He drank some more of his beer.

"Wow," Tori said. "What was it. You know. Like?"

"I don't know," he said. "It happened so fast. They both looked so... surprised. They just stood there. Looking at me. I was so jacked on adrenaline, it was like I was on fast forward and they were on pause. I shot them. They went down. I felt pretty, I don't know. Calm. Later, in Cyrus' car, I got the shakes pretty bad. I had to pull over and spit up something that tasted like battery acid. I got some on my tie, a really nice Ralph Lauren, blue, with gold and maroon geometric patterns. I had to take it off and throw it in a garbage can. After that I was okay."

"David?" she said.

"Yes, Tori?"

"I'm glad they didn't shoot you," she said.

"Thanks, T," he said.

"And David?"

"Yes, Tori?"

"I wasn't really going to shoot you," she said.

"I know," he said, rubbing her hand.

"David?" she said.

"Yes, Tori?"

"You'll... I'll see my mother and get this straightened out, but... you'll help me, won't you? You'll give me my share of the money and the dope so I can get out of this, won't you?"

"Of course I will," he said. "I'll take care of you. There's no need to worry. Everything's going to be just fine."

They sat for a while.

"Honey?" she said.

"Yes, Tori?"

"Honey, would you. Like to. You know. Lie down? With me? For a while? I missed you. I mean, you know, the girls in jail are nice and all. But it's not the same."

33-1/3

Dave walked around the Fenway, relaxing, feeling the sun on his face. There was a game at the park and the neighborhood was full of sports fans and cute little girls walking cute little dogs. He walked past the Rose Garden and watched the ducks paddling around in the pond. It made him hungry. He went to some bar and ate some buffalo wings. He was grateful for the air conditioning. It was a warm day, but he couldn't take off his jacket because he had too many guns on.

The place was full of pretty college girls. In the Army they would have called it a target rich environment. All the girls had on shirts cut short and pants cut low to show their bellies. He couldn't decide if it was the greatest fashion trend ever or cruel and unusual punishment for a guy. Looking at a chick's belly was painfully erotic. The bellies all looked good. Some were flat and showed the time the chicks had spent in the gym. Others were soft, even rolling out a little over the top of the pants, but that looked sexy, too. His dick was getting so hard it felt like he was wearing another gun.

It was pointless trying to stop staring, so he stared. He didn't remember reading about it in the paper, but there seemed to be a new policy that all chicks had to wear blouses so flimsy and tight that you could clearly see their nipples. He could make out every little bump on the nipples of chicks halfway across the room, especially with the air conditioning in this place.

He was really going to have to do something soon about his social life. Maybe it wasn't so impossible after all that he could make it with a normal girl. You can fool some of the people a lot of the time.

He smiled and shook his head. What was he thinking? It would never work. A girl like that would look at his arms and immediately the lectures about drugs would start. If I liked lectures, he would tell her, I would of stayed in school. She wouldn't think that was funny. He'd be single again.

Looking at the chicks, his balls were starting to hurt. He turned toward the wall, stared into his beer, watched the bubbles rise, and tried to figure what he was going to do with Tori. She had left in the morning with his Mercedes and her .38 to go to Roslindale and talk to her mother. He had told her it was a bad idea, that she should stay out of sight. She listened patiently, told him he was right, and went anyway.

He hoped she got the money back from Eileen. Because he had no intention of giving her half or in fact any of the money or the dope. He had stolen it fair and square. He hadn't figured out yet how he was going to talk her out of wanting it. She was hard to talk out of things. He tried to think of a single thing he had ever talked her out of. He couldn't remember any.

He walked back to the hotel. The desk clerk waved to him as he came in.

"Good evening, Mr. King. Mrs. King asked me to tell you she would wait for you in the lounge," he said.

"Mrs. King," Dave said.

"Mrs. King," the clerk said.

"Thank you very much," Dave said. He tried not to be annoyed, but he was annoyed. Going to Roslindale was one thing, but Tori should know better than to sit and drink in a public place at a time like this.

He walked over to the lounge. The entertainment had started. In the hotels where he could afford to stay, the lounge entertainment was usually a teevee showing the news or the Red Sox. It had always seemed to him that a hotel lounge should have sixty-year old black guys in suits, wearing sunglasses and porkpie hats, playing jazz. He would probably find the sax player shooting up in the next stall in the men's room around midnight. He still half hoped, every time he walked into one, that it would be like that.

Of course not. The Sox. He looked around the lounge. Maureen Sheehan was sitting at the bar, drinking a glass of wine. She smiled when she saw him. She was wearing a yellow sundress that showed her shoulders, which were freckled.

"Good evening, Mrs. King," he said, sitting down next to her.

"Good evening, Mr. King," she said. She sounded a little drunk.

"You look... fucking dynamite, Mrs. King," he said.

"Thank you, Mr. King. You are a silver-tongued devil."

She looked at him.

"What's the matter, Mrs. King?"

"No kiss for your wife, Mr. King?" she asked.

He kissed her. Her lips were slightly apart.

"Thank you, Mr. King," she said.

"Thank you, Mrs. King," he said.

"Uh - dear?" he said.

"Yes? Honey?" she said.

"What the fuck are you doing here? Dear?"

"I got sick of waiting for you to answer my goddamn texts. Honey," she said.

"Fuck," he said.

"What?" she said.

"My phone," he said. "Battery."

She laughed.

"You're a piece of work," she said. "Honey. I guess that's why I married you."

"How did you find me?" he asked.

"You, uh, told me?" she said. "When I asked you where you lived? You told me you were staying here for a while. You said it was a long story. I called, but there was no Leo Diamond registered. Or Glen Plaid. I called, but you didn't answer. I drove in from Saugus, and I told the clerk I was looking for my husband. I told him you were a handsome mysterious man with long hair, probably wearing a suit, even though it's too hot. He goes 'Ah! Mr. King!' I go 'Of course, Mr. King!' I did good, huh?"

"Very good," he said. "So what can I do for you tonight? Maureen?"

"Well," she said. "Leo. I'm glad you asked. Listen, you know, you're the detective here, not me. I don't want to tell you how to do your job. I understand these things take time. There's rules you have to follow. Laws you have to obey. But I can't wait any more. I'm going nuts scratching my fucking balls up in Saugus. Waiting for something to happen. Waiting for you to return my fucking calls. I can't stand not knowing. I need to find out what happened to Richie so I can get on with my life, one, you know, way or the other. I don't have to follow any rules and I don't give a shit about any laws. I want to do something and I want to do it tonight."

She looked around the lounge and lowered her voice to a whisper that Dave could feel deep in his lap. "I want to break into Butchie's office. I don't know, I have a feeling there might be some kind of clue there. You can turn me down if you want. I'll go by myself if I have to. But I'd like you to help me."

"I see," he said. "Is that all?"

"No," she said. She leaned over to whisper. "I want some more of those pills you gave me the other day."

78

Dave unlocked the door to his room, opened a beer, and sat down in a chair by the window. He spread a newspaper out on the floor, took the .45 out, and put it on the paper. With a pillowcase from the bed, a can of sewing machine oil, a toothbrush, and a screwdriver, he took the gun apart and cleaned it. He had just wiped down the outside of the frame and was about to put the gun back together when he heard a click. The door opened.

"Hey, partner," Jason said as he walked in. "Sorry if I caught you in the middle of something."

"No problem," Dave said.

"Do me a favor," Jason said, bringing his Glock out from behind his back. "The other one. The magnum in the shoulder holster. Take it out and throw it over onto the bed. I just want to talk to you for a few minutes. I don't want to have to worry about you panicking and somebody maybe getting hurt."

Dave took the magnum out and threw it onto the bed. "What can I do for you, partner?" he asked.

"That's good," Jason said. "Smooth. You're a smooth-talking fuck. A real bullshit artist. I tell you I want to work with you, you say fine. I kill two cops for you, you say don't worry about it, it's fine. Well, it's not fine. I'm sitting at home, thinking, I'm on administrative leave now, because I shot two cops, to save your junkie ass - "

"Strictly speaking," Dave said, "only one of them was an actual cop - "

"Shut up," Jason said. "They were two brother officers. Knights of the Commonwealth of Massachusetts. So I'm home, I'm just sitting there thinking. Thinking how did I get into this mess, how did I end up shooting two cops to help another cop? Then it came to me. You lying sack of shit. You're not a cop. You're some kind of mafia hit man. You went to Butchie's office to try to find out where Richie went so you can find him and whack him over some fucking guinea mob shit. Then I started poking my nose in. And you know what I couldn't figure out?"

"Uh, what?"

"Why you didn't just kill me right away. It was smooth, what you did. You're a smart guy. You didn't want trouble at your place, cops coming in asking questions, so you asked me to come out for a drink with you. To celebrate our being partners. You piece of jack shit. You were going to shoot me down in the street like a fucking dog. Then when those other guys came at us and the place was already a crime scene and you had nothing to lose, you would have shot me right then in that hallway, except because of those stupid old guns you use, you were out of fucking bullets!"

"Jason, I - "

"Shut up!" Jason said. "Shut up. You were going to wait until Internal Affairs was finished with me, then you were going to ask me to meet you somewhere and put a slug behind my ear, weren't you? And I'd come running, thinking you were my buddy, thinking we were partners. Well, partner, I'm not waiting."

He pointed his gun at Dave's face. Tori stepped out of the bathroom, a towel wrapped around her, and put the barrel of her .38 to the back of Jason's head.

"Move and I'll kill you, you fat fuck," she said.

"Hey, T," Dave said.

"Shut up, David," she said. "You, lardass, throw your gun on the bed."

Jason threw his gun on the bed, next to Dave's.

"Now," she said. "Walk slowly over and stand by David."

Jason went and stood by Dave's chair. Dave stood up and started toward the bed where his gun was.

"Stay where you are, David," Tori said. "I'm not finished with you."

"What do you mean?" Dave asked.

"You motherfucker," she said. "You backstabbing cocksucking motherfucking traitor. After everything I did for you, the minute my ass is in jail, you turn around and go into business for yourself?"

"Tori, didn't you hear - "

"Shut up! Shut up! I heard something about partner. That's all I needed to hear. I can't believe it. I can't believe you would do this to me. My friends laughed at me. When I took you on. Cyrus. The Kid. Murphy. They said what do you want to work with a loser like that for? You told me you were a big drug dealer in the Army, but they told me the truth, that you were nothing but a nickel-and-dime errand boy who tried to start his own business and got busted trying to make his first buy. You were nothing. But I thought you were cute and I felt sorry for you, so I let you ride around with me. This job was a gift. Now you do this to me. Now you turn on me like this. Well, it didn't work, David. You made a mistake and you got caught again, you stupid prick."

She pulled back the hammer on the gun. It clicked into place.

"You made a mistake too, T," Dave said.

"What mistake?' she said.

"It's nothing to be embarrassed about," Dave said. "A lot of people make it. Look how Sid Vicious died. You go to jail, you've got no dope, all you do is lay in bed, staring at the ceiling, thinking about dope, dreaming about it. Thinking how big a spoonful you're going to cook up the minute you get out of jail. You forget that you don't have the same tolerance you had before you went in. You can't handle what you used to handle. Last night I waited until you passed out, then I took the gun out of your belt. I know you, T. I knew no matter what I tried to do to help you, I'd be wrong, like I always am with you. So I fucked up your gun. I filed down the firing pin with a file I had from the toolbox in Cyrus' car. Then I put your gun back in your pants. I knew I should have put a pillow over your face and suffocated you myself right then. But because I'm so stupid, such a fucking idiot, such a loser, just like your big-time friends told you, I turned you on your side so if you puked you wouldn't choke on vomit and die. That's what a sap I am. I ought to kill you right now, just for old times' sake. But because I'm such a nice guy, I'm going to give you one last chance to get out of this. You've probably got two seconds to turn and run before Jason wakes up and reaches for his gun. Now you've got one second."

Tori smiled. "You're lying, David," she said. "I can always tell when you're lying."

She started pulling the trigger wildly. The shots boomed like cannon fire in the little room. The television exploded behind Dave. Jason dove sideways onto the bed, his hand closing on the grip of his Glock as he landed. He brought it up and fired four quick shots in a row into Tori's chest. She fell back against the wall. Dave took two steps over to the bed, picked up the magnum, stuck the barrel in Jason's ear, and pulled the trigger. "Asshole!" he whispered, then shot Jason twice more. He walked over to Tori. She had slid down and was lying against the wall. The front of the towel was full of blood. She had already stopped breathing and was staring straight ahead.

"Sorry about that, T," he said.

Her gun had fallen on the rug by her right hand. He looked at it, thinking. That would explain the .38 slugs in the walls and through the teevee. He wiped his own prints off the magnum with his tie and put it into her left hand, closing her fingers on it to make clear prints. That would take care of the magnum slugs in what was left of Jason's head. He walked over to the chair, where the parts of his .45 were laid out on the newspaper on the floor. He was about to fold up the paper and take it with him when he stopped and looked around the room. The cops would find two people who had apparently shot each other, with the guns still in their hands. The angle of the magnum rounds as they had hit Jason wouldn't be exactly right, but the cops would probably let it drop. They'd close the books on the incident. Nobody would be looking for another shooter. But if he left the .45 too, the gun that had killed Cyrus and the Kid, they would figure Jason had done those shootings. Or Tori had. He had just cleaned the .45, so there wouldn't be any of his fingerprints on it. All the guns from the shootings of Cyrus, the Kid, Murphy, Sean, Jason, and Tori would be accounted for. He couldn't be linked to any of it. He could walk away clean.

7-11

Dave sat at the foot of the bed, watching Maureen sleep. He had taken off his jacket and shirt and tie and splashed some water on his face. Private detecting was hard work. He thought about lying down himself.

He looked at Maureen's face as she slept. He didn't know anyone who looked that way. He hadn't seen a face that looked so innocent since he was a kid and had a hamster. As he watched, her eyes opened slowly. She looked at him, then around the room.

"Where am I?" she asked.

"I apologize," he said. "I forget sometimes that everybody's not a pill jockey like me. I shouldn't have given you that many. You started to nod out in the lounge. I got you this room to lie down for a while. You were okay in the elevator, but in the hall you went out like a light. I had to carry you in here."

"Ah," she said. She reached under the sheets and into her panties. "So, ah, we didn't, ah…"

"No," he said. He got up and went to the closet, put his shirt on, and started buttoning the buttons.

"Okay," she said. "After the bar, I don't remember anything. Sometimes when I'm really wasted and I'm with as, you know, you're a handsome guy, I've been known to… you bastard. What's that smile for?"

"Well," he said, looping his tie around his neck. "You did get a little… aggressive. In the elevator on the way up here. Before you passed out. I was tempted, of course, but you were pretty out of it. It wouldn't have been. You know. Professional ethics."

"I'm sorry," she said.

"Sorry?" he said, tying a four-in-hand and pulling the small knot tight against his top button. "Fuck. I'm thinking of giving you fifty percent off my fee. Do that again and you get a hundred percent off."

"It's… I mean, you're a nice… I do think you're… if things were… but this thing… with Richie – "

"You don't have to explain anything to me," he said. He took his jacket from its hanger and put it on.

"What happened to your other guns?" she asked. "That were always poking out of your jacket," she said. "On the side and in the back."

"I, uh, switched," he said. "This weather. It's too hot to keep my jacket on all the time. I got a compact gun that's easier to hide."

He looked at her.

"Are you ready to go?"

"Where are we going?" she said.

"I should take you back to Saugus," he said.

"What about my plan?"

"You remember that," he said.

"Yeah. Of course I fucking remember that. Look at the clock. It's the middle of the night. Those guys work late sometimes, but not this late. It's the perfect time to break into the office."

He said nothing.

"What?" she said. "You don't like my plan? You got a better one?"

"I'm just thinking," he said. "Do we have any, like, specific ideas of what Butchie would have in his files that might help us?"

"Uh, I won't know that?" she said. "Until I look? In the files? Will I? Come on. What kind of tough guy are you?"

They took the back stairs down to the parking lot.

"What are all these cop cars doing here?" she asked.

"I think there was some kind of trouble on one of the other floors earlier," he said. "I heard sirens when I was on my way up to check on you. I figured I'd rest a little myself and we'd wait until things quieted down."

"But what are those cops doing around your car?" she asked.

"Just keep walking," he said. "Don't look. We'll take your car."

Dave drove North on Route 1 in Maureen's Kia. There was hardly anyone on the roads. In the passenger seat, Maureen drank from a cup of Dunkin' Donuts coffee. She had on his suit jacket with the sleeves rolled up.

As he drove, Dave tried to clear his mind and think. The exit to her apartment came before the car lot, so he would have to decide soon if he was going to dump her at her place or go through with this break-in. It had been a bad mistake to let her get coffee. It was waking her up and the pills were wearing off. His plan to take her home and put her to bed with a promise to do the break-in the following night, now that had been a good plan. When she was asleep he could reach behind the garbage pail under her kitchen sink, get the duffel bag with the dope, the money, and the shotgun he had hidden there, slip out, steal another car, and be gone. That plan wouldn't work now. It was too bad. With all the shootings, all the betrayals, all the cops, all the paperwork, it had all piled up. It was too much. It was time for him to leave Boston forever.

"This coffee is doing the trick," she said. "Those pills of yours make me feel like my brain is made of cotton."

"If you're too fucked up to do this tonight – "

"Keep driving," she said. "I wouldn't miss it for the world. The time is just right. I've even had my breakfast. I can't believe you carry bacon around in your jacket. You're a strange guy. Interesting, but strange."

There was that flirtatious talk again. He told himself not to listen. Broads did that shit. It was how they were. The way they looked at things, flirting with a guy they didn't really want was fair play. They needed to show their boyfriend or husband that other men were interested in them and their own guy better shape up or else. Or they needed to prove to themselves that they were still good looking. It was a scam. He told himself he of all people should know a scam when he saw one.

He tried not to think about the way she had felt in his arms as he carried her into the hotel room. The image of her lying down on the bed in that thin cotton dress kept coming back into his mind. It occurred to him that there was only one letter's difference between sundress and undress.

It was too bad he hadn't been able to do anything for Maureen. He wasn't really any farther along in his investigation than he had been when he started. He had no idea what had happened to Richie Pastorio. Granted, it was his first case. No one succeeded at everything their first time out. But he would have liked to help her.

The exit to Maureen's apartment was coming up in a minute or two. He looked over at her.

"What are you thinking?" she asked.

"Nothing," he said. "What are you thinking?"

"I'm thinking about earlier. When I woke up in that hotel room and you were sitting on the bed. In that wife-beater."

"Yeah?"

"I like those shirts. The way they show a guy's shoulders. I think they're really, you know. Manly. I think it's funny that yours has one of those little horsies stitched on it."

"It's Ralph Lauren."

"I know. But don't you think the little horsie is kind of... gay?"

"I don't think so," he said.

"All right," she said. "Don't get all huffy. You asked me what I was thinking."

She drank from her coffee. "And. I was also thinking. About those needle marks. On your arms. I'm not anti-drug. I smoke pot. I just ate a bunch of your pills and I liked it. It's. You know. None of my business. I just wonder, though. What it's, I don't know. Like."

He said nothing.

"You're not going to try to bullshit me, are you?" she said. "Like you're a diabetic or something? I know half the shit you say to me is bullshit, but don't lie to me about this. I saw your arms with my own eyes. Jesus."

"I'm not going to lie," he said. "I just. I don't think anybody's ever really asked me that. It... makes life very..."

"What?" she asked.

"Soft," he said. "Soft. Like everything's fine. And safe. Like nothing bad can happen. I used to worry all the time. When I was younger. About everything. It's been so long now, I don't even know the guy I used to be, who was so worried all the time. And I don't want to know him. Fuck him."

99

Dave pulled into the parking lot of Pastorio Auto Leasing. The fluorescent lights over the car lot were still on, but the office was dark. He pulled the car around behind the office building and shut off the engine.

"Well?" Maureen said.

"Just give me a minute," Dave said. He patted his jacket pockets. "You wouldn't by any chance have a spoon?"

"What?"

"Never mind," he said. He took a chapstick from his jacket pocket. Carefully taking off the cap, he poured a pile of white powder onto the back of his hand, held it up to his nose, and sniffed. He poured out another pile, held it up to his other nostril, and sniffed again, then put the chapstick back in his pocket.

"You really got a problem," she said.

"Not any more," he said. "Let's go."

Maureen tried her key to the office door. It opened. She started going through the papers on Butchie's desk.

Just to be doing something, Dave checked his gun. He took the .25 out of his jacket pocket. It looked like a toy compared to the guns he had been using, but it would have to do. He had cleaned it earlier with some sewing machine oil and a toothbrush. That reminded him. He needed a new toothbrush. He sniffed the barrel. It smelled like oil and steel. It was a homey, comforting smell. Like turkey cooking on Thanksgiving. Or gasoline on the ground at a filling station on a hot summer day. He put the gun back in his pocket.

"How's it going over there, Starsky?" he asked.

"Pretty good, Hutch," she said. "I think I've got something here."

"What is it?"

She turned over some more papers.

"Well..." she said.

"Well?" he said.

"Well," she said. "It looks like Butchie had an audit done to assess the value of the company."

"Like he was going to sell?" Dave asked.

"Could be," she said. "There's another audit here. It's only a couple of days old. For their boat."

"Butchie's liquidating their assets," Dave said.

"It's a lot of money," she said. "Jesus. I should have asked for a bigger raise."

"Maybe him and Richie argued about it," Dave said. "Maybe Richie didn't want to sell."

"Maybe," she said.

"Maybe Butchie wanted all the money," he said. "They say blood is thicker than water."

Maureen looked up at him. "I hate that shit," she said. "What the fuck is that supposed to mean? What does water have to do with blood or anything else?"

"I... good question," he said.

"Fuck me," she said. "This isn't right. Richie was a good guy. Is a good guy. He doesn't deserve to die over a few thousand bucks."

Maureen leafed through some more files. Neither of them heard the quiet footsteps outside the office. Maureen looked up in time to see a figure outside the door.

"Fuck!" she hissed.

Butchie Pastorio pushed open the door and turned on the light. Dave pulled his gun from his jacket pocket. Butchie reached out and grabbed the little automatic out of

Dave's hand, then clubbed him on the forehead with the butt of his own gun. Dave was a little high, so the pain felt far away, like it was happening to somebody else, but from surprise he lost his footing and sat down on the floor with his back against the desk.

Butchie pointed the gun at him. "You. Fucko. You're not a cop," he said. Dave looked up. Butchie's gun had the widest barrel he had ever seen on a handgun. It had to be a .44 magnum.

Butchie looked at Maureen. "Hello, Maureen," he said.

"Hello, Butchie," she said.

"So," Butchie said. "You're looking for my brother. Well. You'll see him soon enough."

187

Dave reached up toward his forehead, but Butchie waved the big magnum at him. Dave let his hand drop. Blood trickled down his forehead, collected in his eyebrow, then dripped into his eye. With his other eye he looked at Butchie. Butchie was wearing a dark green double-breasted silk suit over a black t-shirt. He looked just like a gangster on television. He switched the gun to his left hand, took a cell phone from his jacket pocket, and dialed a number.

"Hey," Butchie said. "Listen, come down to the office. I need you here. Yeah. As soon as you can. All right."

"Why did you do it, Butchie?" Maureen asked. "How could you kill your own brother?"

Butchie said nothing. Dave sifted through his options. If someone else was coming, he had to move fast. The toy red Mercedes was there on the desk, right by his head. If he could reach up and grab it, throw it, hit Butchie in the face with it, it might distract him until Dave could hit him, knock him over, get the gun out of his hand. But Butchie was watching him closely, and was standing too far away for Dave to make a grab at him.

"Maureen," Butchie said. "It's not going to be the same around here without you. The guy I hired to do your job is a sharp kid, but he doesn't have your... spirit. I'm sorry to say he didn't think much of the accounting you did. And he was surprised we didn't have a security system. He ordered all the stuff over the internet and installed it himself. When you open the door here an alarm rings at my place, it calls my phone, and the hidden camera turns on. I have the option to call the cops or not call the cops." He smiled. "That's my favorite part."

Butchie looked from Maureen to Dave and shook his head. Dave tried to stay calm, motionless, so Butchie wouldn't see him getting ready.

"Maureen, Maureen," Butchie went on. "It's a beautiful name, Maureen. I never met anyone named Maureen before. It's... a beautiful name."

"Thank you, Butchie," she said. "That's a nice thing to say."

"Maureen, we're not going to be seeing each other after tonight. There's something I'd like to say to you."

"Go ahead, Butchie," she said. "I'm listening."

Butchie took a deep breath.

"Maureen, I saw the way you looked at my brother. I knew, you know, how you felt. He knew too. He tried to be... careful with you. He always liked you, but not, you know. In that way. Good guy, my brother. Thoughtful guy. He thought too much. That was his problem. Anyway, I thought that maybe with him gone, you might stay working here and over time we could get to know each other better and someday I could tell you... about the. You know. Feelings I had. For you. But I see now that that's not going to happen."

"I never knew, Butchie," she said.

Dave guessed about two minutes had passed since Butchie had hung up the phone. If he was going to make a move it would have to be soon.

"I know," Butchie said. "You were only interested in my brother. Do you know when I knew that I was getting serious about you and I couldn't stop myself? It was the day I came in and found you TurtleWaxing my little toy Mercedes. The one that James Bond here is going to try to throw at me in a minute. I knew that day I had no choice and I was just going to have to ride it out wherever it went. I'm sorry it has to end like this."

They all heard the car pull up outside the office. They heard the door open and close. They heard the footsteps out in the parking lot. Dave looked at Butchie. Butchie looked at Dave. Maureen looked at Dave. Dave looked up at Maureen, then down at the red Mercedes. Maureen looked at the Mercedes, then at Butchie.

"Do me a favor, Maureen," Butchie said. "Leave the fucking Mercedes on the desk. Christ, you people have no fucking class."

Dave realized he had only seconds. If he threw himself at Butchie's legs, knocked him off balance, it would take him a couple of seconds to swing that big heavy gun around. It was a long shot, but Dave might be able to reach into Butchie's jacket pocket, where he had put the .25. He still hadn't test fired it to see if it even worked. But it was the only chance he had.

Butchie looked down at Dave.

"Am I not making myself clear, Mr. Bond?" he asked. "Stay where you are. Or would you prefer if I just fucking kill you right now?"

Butchie took a step forward and stuck the barrel of the .44 into Dave's left eye. Dave could feel the vibration in his eyeball as Butchie pulled the hammer back and tightened his pull on the trigger.

The door of the office opened. A man with a dark tan, wearing a yellow Hawaiian shirt, white linen pants, and sandals walked in. He looked a lot like Butchie. The two of them could almost be brothers.

I-95

"Thanks for coming down, Richie," Butchie said. "Sorry I had to wake you up. This rent-a-cop has been working with Maureen to try to figure out what I did with your body."

Maureen looked like she was going to faint. She sat down in Butchie's chair. Richie looked at her, shaking his head.

"Maureen," he said. "I'm so sorry. I didn't know you were so worried about me. I left in. You know. A hurry. I should have talked to you first. That was a mistake."

"Richie, what the fuck? What happened to you?" she asked.

Richie looked at Butchie.

"You didn't tell her?"

"Tell her what?" Butchie said. "It's your mess. You clean it up. What am I, your fucking nigger?"

Richie looked at Maureen. "I'm sorry, Maureen," he said. "I've been down in Mexico. I needed some time to myself, to think. I didn't know it was going to cause a problem back here."

"Uh, excuse me?" Dave said quietly. "Is there any way you could..."

Butchie took the .44 out of Dave's eye and moved back a few steps. "Sorry," he said.

"Forget it," Dave said, sitting up and rubbing his eyeball.

"Richie," Maureen said, "why didn't you tell me? Why didn't you tell anyone where you were going?"

Richie shrugged. "I don't know. I was. I was embarrassed."

"Why?" she asked.

"I can't believe Butchie didn't tell you anything," Richie said.

"Blow me," Butchie said.

"It was... fuck me, man," Richie said. "It's about my life."

"What about it?" Maureen said.

"My life is good," he said. "I mean, look at me. I'm successful. I got money. I got my hair. I still get plenty of young trim. Excuse my French."

"So?" Maureen said.

"So," Richie said, "I started asking myself. If my life is so great, why can't I sleep, why does food taste like newspaper to me, why can't I stop thinking about putting an HK in my mouth?"

"What's an HK?" Maureen asked.

"It's a top-of-the-line German handgun," Dave said.

"Shut up," Butchie said.

"Well?" Maureen said.

Richie looked around. "Listen," he said, "hold on one minute, okay?"

Richie walked out the door into the parking lot. They heard a car door open and close. He came back with a six-pack of Bud tallboys. He gave a can to Butchie, one to Maureen, and one to Dave. Dave held the cold can against the bruise on his forehead.

"Can you believe this fucking guy?" Butchie asked Maureen. "One of a kind, my brother."

Richie drank from his beer. "Thanks, Butch," he said.

"So," Richie continued, "Anyways."

"Richie, Maureen said. "Please just tell me. You're fucking killing me here."

"Okay," he said. "Okay. So. Anyways. I get up one morning. It's the morning after you were here and. You know. Looked after me. I never told you. You know. How much I... Jesus. Anyways, I've been awake all night anyway, thinking I can't do this another day. I got to do something, about, you know, my life, like, today, or I'm going to get my HK and put one through the roof of my mouth. I drive to the airport. I get a plane down to Cancun. I figure why not? I always liked the sun and the water. I'm thinking maybe it might help me do something about my mood. Give me a chance to think. If not, I figure I'll just walk down to the beach, swim out until I can't swim any more, and that'll be that."

"So," she said.

"So the first day I go and sit out on the beach. It's nice. The sun. The water. But I don't care. It's too late. I'm done. I decide I'm going to swim out and drown myself. But I gotta wait until there's nobody on the beach, no one to see me, to try to save me. Well, fuck me if I can get a minute to myself all goddamn day. A kid from one of the hotels is selling beers in an ice chest. It's hot. I'm thirsty. I buy a couple of beers.

Some young kids come up and start talking to me. Australians. They say they can tell I'm a yank. I'm thinking great, I'm getting called a jerkoff the one fucking time I'm not carrying a gun. Then I figure it out. Yank. They mean American."

"That's funny," Dave said.

"Shut up," Maureen said.

"Yank," Richie said, shaking his head. "So, I talk to them for a while. I tell them about mine and Butch's business. Then I ask them what they do. They laugh in my face. They don't do a goddamn thing. They're Australians. They save up their money and they travel around the world, for, like, years. They camp. Sleep on the beach. Maybe make friends somewhere and stay at their houses for a while, or pick up some chickenshit work here or there. Bartending. Picking grapes in Spain or olives in Italy. They don't have a thing in the world to worry about. I'm sitting there listening to them talking about it, and I'm about to start crying like a fucking girl. I've never heard anything so... beautiful."

He was quiet for a minute.

"I hang out with them for about a week. We sit on the beach. Drink some beers. Swim. Hike. I buy some sunscreen while I still have some skin left. And even though we're doing stuff all the time, I feel like it's the first chance I've had in years to really think. I'm the oldest in our family. I took over the business from my Pop. It was expected. I never wanted to compete with Butchie, so when he got old enough, we started running things together. It was a good system. It worked. Now I see that Butch is better at this work than me. He likes it better. He doesn't need me here. And I don't want to be here. So. Fuck it. I'm going on walkabout, like those Australian kids. I'm going to take our boat and go I don't even know where. I'm buying out Richie's half."

"I keep telling him he can have it," Butchie said.

"It makes me feel better," Richie said. "I don't know why. I just want to feel like things are settled for me here. Then I'm heading south. Follow the sun, you know?

Maybe it sounds, I don't know. Stupid. Maybe life's not about being happy. But. I don't know. What's it supposed to be about. I don't know. Nobody ever told me. So I'm going to try. What do I got to lose? You know what I mean?"

"So," Maureen said. "You're going by your-"

"I'm taking one of the Australian kids with me," Richie said. "To – you know. Help me sail the boat. I don't even really know how to sail. Butchie always drove when we took it out."

Butchie laughed. "Can you believe this fucking guy? One in a million."

Maureen asked "So… where is this… kid now?"

Richie looked at the floor. "I flew her up here with me," he said.

No one said anything.

"That's good, Richie," Maureen said quietly. "I'm glad for you. So that's that. I mean that's why you came back. Here. To get the boat."

Richie looked at Butchie.

"That's one reason. But I had to come back anyway. The cops took you serious, Maureen. They thought maybe Butchie whacked me and buried me at the back of the lot. They've been questioning him and the rest of our family. And our family... how does it go, Butch?"

Butchie smiled. "Our family places a high premium on privacy."

"We never used to have any problem with the cops," Richie said. "We had the Chief of Detectives in Saugus on our payroll, and he always kept them away from our loansharking and narcotics and - "

"Rich," Butchie said. "They don't need to know this much about our business."

"Whatever," Richie said. "Anyways, they wanted to see me in person. To make sure I was still alive. I came back for a few days to straighten things out. And there's something I want to talk about with you, Maureen."

"Richie, you don't have to – "

"With Butchie handling things here and me taking some time off, the thing is, I'm interested in maybe investing some of my money, letting it work for me while I'm gone. I was thinking about the hotel business. I remember you told me the night, you know, before I left, that you were interested in hotel management yourself. So I was wondering if you might be willing to act as sort of an agent for me and buy a bed and breakfast place. I can advance you whatever cash you need for a trip up North to find a place you think is a good investment. When you do, you let Butchie know and he'll get in touch with me and we'll buy it for you. You'd really be doing a big favor for me personally if you could do this. Taxes and shit. So. What do you say?"

"Thank you, Richie," she said quietly. "I'd be glad to help."

99

Dave, Maureen, and the Pastorio brothers walked out onto the lot. The sky was changing slowly from deepest black to darkest blue.

"It's going to be warm," Butchie said. "So Rich, when are you going in to meet with the cops?"

"Later this morning," Richie said. "Jesus, is that crazy about Jason or what?"

"Unbefuckinlievable," Butchie said. "Shot in a hotel room. By some junkie broad."

"Christ almighty," Richie said. "At this rate, pretty soon we won't have any employees left."

Dave and Maureen got into her car and drove to her place. Neither of them said anything. As they came in her front door they could see the sun coming up through the living room window. He opened two cans of beer and gave her one. They sat on the couch.

"I'm beat," she said. "I could sleep for a week."

"Why don't you lie down for a while?" he said.

"Too tired," she said.

He drank from his beer.

"So," he said. "What now?"

"I don't know," Maureen said. "Le – now, come on. I can't call you Leo Diamond. Your real name can't be that bad."

He smiled.

"My name is David Fontaine," he said.

"Well, David," she said. "I don't know what to think. I don't know how I feel. This bed and breakfast... thing... it's what I've dreamed of doing for a long time. You know. Cook waffles. Wear sweaters with, like, reindeers on them. Get some dogs. But this isn't the way I imagined getting it. I mean, I guess I earned it, in a way. But I feel. I don't know. Like a whore."

She looked at him.

"What about you?" she asked.

"I feel the same way," he said.

"That's not what I meant," she said. "I mean do you have a dream?"

"Yeah," he said.

"Well," she said. "What is it?"

He was quiet for a minute.

"I've never told this to anybody in my life," he said. "My dream is to... play the saxophone."

"You like jazz?" she asked.

"Not really," he said. "I just like the saxophone."

"That's a good dream," she said. "You know, most people's dreams are like that. Things they really could do if they weren't afraid to try."

She had a point, Dave thought. Look at how well his dream of being a private detective was going.

"Do you like dogs?" she asked.

"Afraid of them," he said. "And they get hair on my suits."

She nodded. They were quiet for a few minutes.

"Look," she said. "Come with me. I never bought a bed and breakfast before. I could really use some help with this. It'll be good for you. You can get out of the city, get off drugs – "

He looked at her, his expression blank.

"All right," she said. "Don't get off drugs. None of my business. I looked in that bag you stashed under the sink. I don't know anything about drugs, but the stuff in there looks like it could keep Saugus and Swampscott and Peabody fucked up for ten years. Anyways, never mind that. You'll really be helping me out. You don't have to stay any longer than you want. Just until I get set up. I'm scared, okay? I'd like you to be there to help me. We'll get you a saxophone. My mom learned to play the piano from videos. You can learn the sax. You want to make your dream come true, don't you? Come on. Say you'll do it. Don't make me beg."

"All right. Fuck it," he said. "I'll do it."

She smiled and yawned. Dave started to ask if he could borrow a spoon, but she was already asleep.

THE END

Made in the USA
Monee, IL
27 May 2020